In Pious Memory

In Pious Memory

by

MARGERY SHARP

LITTLE, BROWN AND COMPANY · BOSTON · TORONTO

FIRST AMERICAN EDITION
PRINTED IN THE UNITED STATES OF AMERICA

11563

To Geoffrey Castle

In Pious Memory

1

AFTER SOME THIRTY years of marriage Mrs. Prelude's sole manifestation of independence was always, when travelling by plane, to sit in the tail. She and her husband flew a good deal; he was an authority on international banking, much in demand wherever his European colleagues gathered in conference, and though austerely avoiding all attendant junketings—receptions, or visits to historic monuments—invariably took Mrs. Prelude along to look after him at the hotel. He suffered from asthma. His giant intellect was housed in but an average body—indeed rather below average; average only in the sense of being unremarkable: all the more startling therefore was the effect when on rostrum or at banquet board he suddenly rose to his feet and let his intellect loose like a lion from a mouse-trap. Mrs. Prelude naturally never witnessed this transformation herself, she was always at home in the hotel bedroom sterilizing his inhaling-apparatus with water boiled over a portable methylated-spirit stove; but other wives told her about it. "Honey, you should have been *there!*" once cried Mrs. van Hoyt—a charming impetuous American whom Mrs. Prelude often met so to speak on circuit. "He just *slayed* even the French!" "Arthur likes to find me waiting for him," explained Mrs. Prelude. "I guess it's a privilege in a way," said Corinna van Hoyt, "to have a man of genius so dependent on you." "Indeed it is," said Mrs. Prelude.

Besides the inhaling-apparatus and the methylated-spirit stove the Preludes' luggage regularly included two special anti-asthma pillows and a supply of special yoghurt to be deposited in the hotel refrigerator immediately upon arrival. What with Arthur's equally indispensable dinner-jacket and tails there would have been excess baggage to pay, if Mrs. Prelude put in evening-dress and wrap. Fortunately she didn't need to; one thin silk dress (for Rome), or of light-weight wool (Stockholm) sufficed, and Arthur was very understanding when she had to buy an umbrella at The Hague.

Many another giant intellect (such as Mr. van Hoyt, whose wife always referred to him as the Prof) greatly envied Arthur Prelude. He had in fact married recklessly early, while still a junior lecturer at the London School of Economics. —His eye caught by a pale pretty student pencilling earnestly in the front row, as he left the dais Arthur glanced at the open page of her note-book; it was covered with sketches of rabbits. Possibly he recognized at that moment a gentle, unambitious nature corollary to his own; in any case he married her, that pale pretty student, and even after the birth of two daughters and a son had never cause to doubt where her true allegiance lay.

All the same, whenever they travelled by plane Mrs. Prelude sat in the tail, even if Arthur couldn't find a place beside her. She'd read somewhere that it was safer, in the tail, and events proved her right. When the jet taking them back from Geneva crashed into an Alp, Mrs. Prelude, in the tail, was but shocked and bruised, whereas of her husband there remained but the remains.

2.

The next forty-eight hours passed to Mrs. Prelude in a sort of dream. Complete strangers were very kind; a nun—in hospital, in a nunnery?—brought her a tisane and advised prayer. "How pretty," murmured Mrs. Prelude, "your white wings! Like the wings of a dove . . ." A doctor (presumably) gave her a tablet that made her sleep; then turned into a courteous, worried official of the air-line. "Madame has no one she wishes summoned?" enquired the courteous, worried official. Mrs. Prelude distinctly recalled her daughters Elizabeth and Lydia and her son William, but couldn't for the life of her remember where they were holidaying. "I suppose there aren't any bankers about?" she asked. "Do not for a moment trouble about money," reassured the official. "I was thinking of the van Hoyts," explained Mrs. Prelude. "But of course they were flying on to Athens. But why should I summon anyone? I'm sure I can get home alone."

The official looked at her compassionately.

"There is first the matter of the identification, madame . . ."

3.

Again it was like a dream, as on the arm of the nun, shepherded by some other official—the British Consul?—Mrs. Prelude was led—in a hospital, in a mortuary?—towards one of a row of still, sheeted figures. Only the head was unshrouded for her; Mrs. Prelude took one swift, agonized glance and looked away even as she nodded through her tears. Then she had to sign something, and everyone was even kinder, particularly the undertaker, who assured her, if not in so many words, that Mr. Prelude would travel perfectly. Mrs. Prelude paid the bill, appropriately, by traveller's cheque; and only then suddenly remembered William's address at a fishing village in Cornwall. He was beside her within a day of receiving her cable, and took her home at once—not by air, however; by rail and sea. "I wouldn't mind," said Mrs. Prelude bravely, "if I could sit in the tail?" But with a coffin, the older way was easier.

4.

The death of such a man as Arthur Prelude naturally caused some stir. His obituary in *The Times* measured five and a half inches; telegrams of condolence, also unwieldy floral tributes, flowed in from heads of banks all over the world. There were fewer personal condolences, he had led too dedicated a life to have much time for private relationships; accordingly few mourners were expected at the funeral, which took place at Chesham Bois in Buckingham-

shire on the morning of June the fourth. The table in the dining-room was spread with but a dozen plates of ham and tongue and one of muesli for a vegetarian executor.

"Thirteen," said Elizabeth uneasily.

She had just finished pulling down the blinds. The coffin wasn't actually in the house, but at the undertaker's—or rather was expected at any moment in the undertaker's hearse, so that Mr. Prelude might set out on his last journey, as convention demanded, from his rightful rate-payer's address. Elizabeth had remembered the blinds only just in time; now, in the sudden gloom, the dining-room had a ghostly look, like a stage-set without lights.

"Take one away," said William. "In fact, take two away. The Wilfreds won't come—not on Toby's last Fourth."

In family parlance this was explicit enough. The Wilfreds—the Wilfred Preludes—were Arthur Prelude's brother and sister-in-law, whose son Toby would leave Eton at the end of that term. He was no common youth, he was in fact Captain of Boats, and upon Eton's gala-day not only enjoyed but reflected a prestige rarely enjoyed by cabinet ministers. There had never been any expectation of Toby's attending his uncle's funeral, and William's guess that his parents wouldn't either was almost immediately confirmed by the arrival of a further telegram.

TERRIBLY DISTRESSED BUT QUITE IMPOSSIBLE ALL LOVE AND SYMPATHY, read William.

"Tell Mother," said Elizabeth.

William hesitated.

"She's still crying . . ."

"Well, of course," said Elizabeth. "Mother's of her gen-

[7]

eration. She behaved quite marvellously, after the crash, and if she's been crying ever since, it's only natural."

"As it's natural for us to remain dry-eyed?"

"I suppose so," said Elizabeth. "After all, we didn't know Father very well."

"If at all," said William, "apart from his appearance and his reputation. Is it usual, do you think?"

"In England, quite," said Elizabeth. "Ever since the Tudors haven't we shocked foreigners by our lack of family warmth? What I feel chiefly—" She paused, considering her words; she had inherited something of her parent's academic brain, and at twenty-eight was a lecturer herself, in Greek, at a London women's college. "What I feel chiefly," stated Elizabeth, "apart from being terribly sorry for Mother, is a sort of anger that Father should have died so . . . wastefully, with years of good work left in him. What do you feel?"

William paused in turn. In him too the academic tradition was strong; though flighting out into the antique trade, he was engaged to the daughter of his tutor at Oxford.

"Very much the same. Lydia, on the other hand, *has* been crying."

"Lydia is sixteen, and dramatizes," said Elizabeth, rather sharply. "Is Mother crying very much?"

"Passionately," said Lydia, from the stairs.

She descended them with a slow and solemn step, but still looked even younger than her years; young enough to slide down the banisters. Her mother-of-pearl finger-nails terminated the thin scratched hands of a child who has been blackberrying; so was her next remark, the great word *passionately* out, equally childish. "How odd everything looks," added Lydia, "with the blinds down! It feels like being in an aquarium."

"Hush!" said Elizabeth.

"Or in a theatre just before the play begins. Or in a haunted house."

"Hush," repeated Elizabeth. "Here's Mother."

Mrs. Prelude had indeed at last emerged from her room. She wore a black silk dress (Rome) under a black woolen jacket (Stockholm), and a small black international hat. But no crepe-bordered Victorian weeds could have made her state of widowhood more explicit; it was explicit in her face—at once white and red-lidded, puffy from weeping and drawn by sorrow. Her hands were shaking, her foot on the stair stumbled; Lydia turned back, William ran up, to support her.

"Are you sure, Mother, you ought to come?" asked Elizabeth anxiously. "Even though it's Father's funeral, if William and Lydia and I are there—"

Mrs. Prelude pressed a handkerchief to her lips. Looking past her children her eye lighted upon an immense laural wreath (misdirected, it should have gone to the undertaker's), inscribed upon a necessarily broad ribbon HOMMAGES DE LA PART DES BANQUES INDUSTRIELLES DE L'INDOCHINE. It seemed to steady her.

"Of course I'm coming," said Mrs. Prelude. "I've never failed in my duty to your father yet . . ."

Also at that moment the hearse arrived, and behind it a large black limousine (once the property of Queen Mary), for the family. When vehicles such as these draw up before a door no delay is possible, they cannot be kept waiting like taxis. Upon William's arm—as upon the arm of the nun—

Mrs. Prelude took her place; Elizabeth and Lydia followed. A second car provided by the undertaker was empty save for two inexplicable Japanese, and actually no one but his immediate family and Arthur Prelude's executor came back to eat the ham and tongue and muesli.

5.

It was wonderful what a difference pulling up the blinds again made. Only those of Mrs. Prelude's bedroom remained drawn; she had gone upstairs to lie down. ("You shouldn't have given her so much brandy," said Elizabeth. "All through the funeral I thought she was going to faint," William defended himself.) Under the sun pouring in through opened windows the dining-table with its several untouched plates had now an almost raffish look, as of an abandoned table d'hôte. Elizabeth emptied the last of the Chablis into her glass, William picked up a slice of ham and ate it between his fingers. "Who'd have thought," said William, "the old man had so much money in him?"

"Well, he was a banking expert," said Elizabeth.

"You don't mean he fiddled in foreign currency?"

"Certainly not," said Elizabeth, "but he must have seen which way a cat was going to jump."

"I must say he left a very fair will," mused William, picking up a slice of tongue. "Speaking as the single male, I hope you appreciate my generosity: I expected more sex-discrimination."

"Father was also a mathematician," said Elizabeth. "Four into eighty thousand goes with a certain beautiful classic simplicity. I shall spend a couple of months in Greece."

"I, you may as well know it now," said William, "shall get married. I've yearned long enough."

"Alice?" said Elizabeth, rather dryly.

"Naturally Alice. Any comment?"

"Only that you'd better stop her driving that absurd jeep," said Elizabeth, "before she either breaks her neck in it or rams a Rolls-Royce."

"Cat," said William, without rancour. —"Lydia of course can't touch capital till she's twenty-one, but if there's anything she wants to train for, funds will be undoubtedly forthcoming. —I suppose it'll be drama-school?"

Lydia nodded blissfully—already remote upon a balcony in Verona.

"The Juliet of the age," said William, not unkindly. "What about Mother?"

"Mother will go and live at Hove," said Elizabeth. "She's always had a hankering after Hove, only Father thought it bad for his asthma. If she takes a nice big flat, and why not, you and Lydia can go for week-ends, and the Wilfreds and Toby in the summer, and at other times her old bids she went to school with and Father couldn't stand."

"I might get into the Brighton rep," said Lydia dreamily.

"And William can poke about the Lanes."

"Not I," said William, "for a cracked Chelsea shepherd-ess ticketed like Ming. But I wouldn't mind poking about Sussex a bit, and dropping in for lunch with Mother by the way. In fact I agree with Elizabeth: I can see myself and my wife quite frequently dropping in for lunch with Mother at Hove."

"And we'll be able to have lobster," said Lydia, in much the same dreamy tone. "Why was lobster bad for asthma?"

"Why were oysters?" countered William.

"Hush!" said Elizabeth.

—As suddenly as she'd appeared on the stair, in the doorway now reappeared Mrs. Prelude. She was no longer pale, however, but flushed, for William had indeed given her too much brandy. She still wasn't half-seas over; only a little voluble, her tongue at last loosed.

"What were you all chattering about?" demanded Mrs. Prelude. "I could hear you from upstairs, chattering and chattering. Chattering and chattering!" repeated Mrs. Prelude.

Her three children exchanged guilty glances. William and Lydia could but hope that their mother hadn't actually distinguished the words *oyster* and *lobster*.

"I'm very sorry, Mother," said Elizabeth, "but we *were* chattering. I know it must seem terribly heartless, just after Father's funeral—"

Once again Mrs. Prelude pressed a handkerchief to her lips; but this time almost immediately dropped it.

"If it *is* your father's," said Mrs. Prelude.

2

ELIZABETH SPOKE FIRST.

"What do you mean, Mother, *if?*" she asked sensibly, but putting her arm round Mrs. Prelude's shoulder. "Of course it's Father's! Whose else could it be?"

"Well, there was a whole row," said Mrs. Prelude.

Her manner, rather alarmingly, was now far more collected. She spoke as reasonably as Elizabeth. —Her children, hitherto but startled, realized with increasing dismay that their mother's grotesque fantasy demanded to be taken seriously.

"But, Mother, you identified him," said William. "Before I flew out, you'd identified him."

"I know," said Mrs. Prelude. "So would you have."

"Then if William would have identified him too," said Elizabeth, "don't you see, Mother, there can't possibly be any doubt?"

"I mean if William had been me," said Mrs. Prelude. —She paused, briefly struggling against fresh tears; also withdrawing herself from her daughter's embrace. "It was all so dreadful and pathetic—"

"Poor Mother!" cried Lydia.

"—I just wanted to get away. I'm not sure now that I

really looked at your father at all—if it was your father. I can't remember looking; that is, I can't remember what he looked like . . ."

"That's the shock," explained Elizabeth, "making you a little lose your memory. We all think you behaved quite marvellously, Mother, but the shock must have been appalling. But now you've told us, and after a good night's sleep—"

"I don't want to go to sleep," said Mrs. Prelude annoyedly. "I want to talk about it. It's no help telling you, if you won't talk about it. And if I *have* made this terrible, terrible mistake, I feel I shall never sleep again."

William, under the urgent eye of Elizabeth, drew a deep breath.

"Listen, Mother," he said, "it's not possible. Just supposing, theoretically, you did make a mistake, when all the other bodies were identified there'd be Father . . . well, left over, and someone else a body short."

"Unless *they* didn't look properly either," said Mrs. Prelude. "I'm sure I wouldn't be at all surprised."

There was a certain logic about this not easy to answer. Her glance at William now one of warning, Elizabeth grasped the nettle.

"Listen, Mother—" (so every sentence her children directed at Mrs. Prelude now began: *Listen, Mother*)— "even if it *is* possible, and that Father's buried somewhere in Switzerland—"

"One coffin was being flown to West Point," recalled Mrs. Prelude.

"—or even at West Point, does it really matter? No one can say he hasn't been paid every due respect."

[*14*]

"He may even have had military honours," cooperated William.

"He was a pacifist," pointed out Mrs. Prelude, "and we still ought to send the wreaths back. With little notes."

For an appalled moment William contemplated an undertaking so complex, macabre and multilingual, his imagination was hypnotized by it. No fewer than twenty-seven floral tributes heaped Mr. Prelude's grave; and while Les Banques Industrielles de l'Indo-Chine could presumably be addressed in French, the tribute from Saudi Arabia was nationalistically dedicated in Arabic, and William felt pretty sure his father wouldn't want to offend the Saudi Arabians by replying as from the grave in Queen's English. The West Berliners, for that matter, also the Dutch, Swedes and Japanese, had paid Mr. Prelude the compliment of lamenting him in their own tongues. "Berlitz?" thought William wildly. At the moment it seemed the answer. A session at Berlitz, and a corps of Special Messengers, each humping to appropriate Embassy or Consulate what would probably be but a skeleton of florist's wire, might do the trick; but though Berlitz could notoriously translate anything, there would first have to be something to translate . . .

"William!" said Elizabeth sharply. "Of course Mother doesn't mean it!"

"You don't seem to understand what I mean at all," complained Mrs. Prelude. "I might be talking to deaf adders. Haven't you realized—"

"I have!" cried Lydia. "Darling, *I* have!"

"Realized what, Mother?" asked Elizabeth.

"There were injured, you know, as well," said Mrs.

Prelude. "Perhaps some of *them* lost their memories, as you say I have. Don't you see, if it *isn't* your father—"

"Listen, Mother—" began William and Elizabeth together—and now with a fresh urgency. But Mrs. Prelude wasn't to be halted.

"—he may be still *alive?*"

2.

All that broke the silence immediately following was the dining-room clock striking three. It was a presentation clock, subscribed for by Arthur Prelude's colleagues after his brilliant handling of a sterling crisis: its expensive chimes rang out punctually, mellifluously, and so to speak pointedly . . .

"But then what d'you think's happened to him, Mother?" asked William, taking he hoped a fresh grip on the situation.

"Perhaps he just wandered off," said Mrs. Prelude, "and some kind-hearted person took him in . . ."

"Monks," said Lydia eagerly. "With St. Bernard dogs. Or simple peasants."

"They'd have to be more than simple, they'd have to be Yetis," said Elizabeth, "not to know about the crash and get in touch with the air-line."

"Yetis?" repeated Mrs. Prelude—beginning to totter.

"Abominable Snowmen," said William.

At which moment Mrs. Prelude fortunately collapsed again, she passed out, and Elizabeth and Lydia were able to take her upstairs and put her finally to bed.

[*16*]

3.

"Of course it's Father," said Elizabeth, returning.

"Also pure Freud," said William. "Even to forgetting where I was until he was safely screwed down—and waiting, here, until after the funeral to unburden herself. Hence the guilt-complex."

"You are saying more than you intend," said Elizabeth, "at least, I hope so. You're saying Mother wanted Father to be dead."

"You've never packed his inhaling-apparatus," said William. "I had to buy a gunny-sack. Hence, as I say, the guilt-complex, following on wish-fulfillment. We must all be very kind to Mother, and find her that flat in Hove at once."

"You are taking it too lightly," said Elizabeth. "*We* may be certain it's Father, but until Mother is, she won't know a moment's peace."

"Who said all she needed was a good night's sleep?" countered William—but uneasily.

"Only a fool never changes his mind," quoted Elizabeth. "It's got to be proved to her."

William hesitated.

"The only way I can see, for absolute proof, though naturally one flinches from it, is to get an exhumation order. It shouldn't be difficult, with a doctor's certificate to say Mother's mental health is at stake."

"As it is," said Elizabeth.

"At least the headstone isn't up. Obviously one couldn't

ask Mother herself to look again, but if you and I identify him—"

Elizabeth shuddered.

"Mayn't there be—well, change and decay?"

"That's sheer cowardice, and you know it."

"Not sheer," said Elizabeth, "though I admit to feeling sick just thinking of it. It's that I don't want to see Father dead and decayed, I want to remember him alive—setting off with his brief-case, full of slightly ridiculous importance—only it wasn't ridiculous, only to us, rather endearingly, because he really was a great man. As a family, we were rather the hero's valet," said Elizabeth frankly, "but that's how I want to remember him—alive."

"D'you suppose I'm going to enjoy digging Dad up?" enquired William bitterly.

"No," admitted Elizabeth. "That's why you want me there with you."

"I shall feel just as sick as you will," said William. "Also rather like a ghoul. If there was anyone else who could identify him—"

"But there is," said Lydia.

4.

Her brother and sister turned on her a common look of surprise mingled with scepticism. They knew all too well Lydia's romantic, active imagination, from the deeps of which, they suspected, she was now about to produce a Middle European mistress or even a bastard son. But they were wrong.

"There's Father's dentist," said Lydia. "Dentists can always identify bodies, the police call them in specially, by their teeth."

"By gum!" said William. —"I'm sorry, I wasn't being funny."

"No one thought you were," said Elizabeth. But the snub was automatic; a mere familiar reaction. She paused, her fine academic forehead clouding. "Who *was* Father's dentist? Do we know?"

"Mr. Hambury-White," said Lydia. "He does me too. His number's Welbeck oh-oh-four-one."

Still Elizabeth paused. Nor did William spring to the telephone. The line was indeed often engaged, but in neither of them appeared any furious impatience.

"I still," said Elizabeth slowly, "as William says, flinch. He and I practically desecrating Father's grave would be bad enough, but to have a dentist poking about his jaw-bone seems to me the last indignity. How do you feel, William?"

"Much the same," admitted her brother. "I've in fact been rather big and brave; I do still feel a sense of . . . desecration."

"Almost of impiety," said Elizabeth. "It's odd how the old myths persist."

"I don't believe a word of either of you," said Lydia, "about desecration and impiety; and Elizabeth never remembered father's brief-case before. *I* know why William would feel like a ghoul, and both of you sick, and a dentist be the last indignity. It's in case Mother's right, and it *isn't* Father."

5.

"That child should be in bed too," said William.

"Of course she should," agreed Elizabeth, "after so much emotion. Poor little Lydia, come and let me tuck you up!"

"If you and William won't get an exhumation order, I shall," said Lydia.

"You're still under-age," reminded William. "If Elizabeth and I object—as we would, wouldn't we, Elizabeth?"

"Certainly," said Elizabeth. "I don't mind admitting that I've changed my mind again. The less horrible fuss that's made the better; we must accept, and help Mother to accept, the facts. Father died in an air-crash; it was tragic, as I've said it was a meaningless waste, but the fact remains. That Mother has a certain Freudian sense of guilt I agree with William is possible—actually it's the only explanation—but the best way we can help her get over it is by behaving completely normally."

"If necessary," said William, "I'm prepared to tell a thumping lie. I'll tell Mother, and say I didn't tell her before to spare her feelings, that I had Father unscrewed in Switzerland and identified him on the spot. —Because obviously it's Father," said William.

"Obviously," said Elizabeth. "It's the truth. —Do you hear, Lydia?"

"You and William," said Lydia doggedly, "are treating me like a child."

"Then stop behaving like one. Don't you see how absolutely essential it is," said Elizabeth, more kindly, "to set poor Mother's mind at rest?"

"Yes, I see that," said Lydia. She paused; it seemed to have been to choose a deliberately childish phrase in which to make the promise implicitly required of her. "All right; I won't tell."

"Then go up to Mother now, William," said Elizabeth.

6.

Her son's confession indeed brought such comfort to Mrs. Prelude, she not only slept the whole night through but woke next morning with apparently no recollection either of having heard it, or of having needed to. —Was it Freud again, or was it alcohol? Mrs. Prelude certainly had a headache. "William gave me too much brandy," she apologized. "I remember coming downstairs, but did I talk too much, was I very silly?"

"You were just upset," said Elizabeth. "Weren't we all, after Father's funeral?"

—She held her breath, ready to comfort and reason and reassure again; there was no need.

"How lovely the wreaths were!" recalled Mrs. Prelude.

"Another's just come in," said Elizabeth, "from Portugal."

"Banco Maritime y do Nova Zembla?" asked Mrs. Prelude eagerly. "We must have it put with the rest; your father always had a feeling, for the Portuguese . . ."

3

ELIZABETH'S POLICY of complete normality in fact
    proved a complete success. —She carried it so far,
she stayed at home only a few days before returning to
academic duty in London, and encouraged William, who
was employed at Sotheby's, to do the same. Lydia, under
protest, was dispatched to finish the term at boarding-
school. But since Mrs. Prelude obviously couldn't be left
quite alone, Elizabeth summoned two of the afore-men-
tioned old bids to bear her company and this turned out the
wisest course possible. To both Miss Champney and Miss
Hume (the one an upaid Liberal agent, the other currently
clipping poodles), the immediate comforts of Chesham
Bois were scarcely less welcome than the prospect of free
holidays at Hove; their reserves of sympathy were inex-
haustible. They could sympathize with Mrs. Prelude (as
Elizabeth was perfectly aware that she and William could
not) eight hours a day. Both also happened to have a taste
for shellfish, and Mrs. Prelude was so grateful to them for
coming to her in her wretchedness, not only the bill at the
fishmonger's soared, but that at the wine-merchant's: one
of the few pieces of information she'd picked up in Stockholm being that any unwholesomeness in shellfish could

always be corrected by a glass of schnapps. Naturally she didn't offer Harriet and Barbara spirits, in fact Mrs. Prelude herself didn't believe shellfish unwholesome at all; but in deference to her late husband's opinion she never served lobster without at least Chablis as an antidote.

It made for a certain cosiness.

Miss Champney, the younger bid, had actually sat alongside Mrs. Prelude at the London School of Economics, and so was particularly qualified to sympathize.

"How well I remember him, your Arthur, on the platform!" sighed Miss Champney. "Could *you* keep up with him? *I* couldn't."

"I'm afraid I just drew rabbits," confessed Mrs. Prelude.

"But won his heart," sighed Miss Champney. (A phrase neither Elizabeth nor William, nor even Lydia, could have brought themselves to utter, but which was just what Mrs. Prelude needed.) "Barbara, you can't *imagine* the sensation! It was like—well, not exactly like King Cophetua and the beggar-maid—"

"But it was," said Mrs. Prelude earnestly. "I was as surprised as anyone. I couldn't believe my luck."

Her friends were not insincere enough to protest that the luck had all been Arthur's, and Mrs. Prelude didn't expect them to. All three had reached nubility at a period when after the First World War the balance of sexes so severely dipped, the term "surplus woman" was a current phrase and to marry at twenty luck indeed. No such luck had come the way of Harriet and Barbara even in their thirties or forties. Miss Champney knew she was far brainier than Mrs. Prelude, and Barbara had quite a standing in the dog-world; but their hostess was a widow, i.e., had been the chosen of a male when males were in short supply. The prestige was sufficient in itself, and they had no need to be insincere to pay their scot.

"And what an interesting life you've had," envied Barbara frankly, "going to all those conferences!"

"Arthur never left me behind," agreed Mrs. Prelude modestly.

"Weren't you terribly proud, when he made all those wonderful speeches?"

"At Geneva, he slayed even the French," said Mrs. Prelude.

"I always thought his most important speech was at The Hague," said Miss Champney, "on the metric system. Actually I know Den Hague quite well."

"Venice is *my* love," confessed Barbara.

For of course they'd both been abroad themselves. (Few English spinsters of a certain class are without a foreign passport.) Actually Harriet was a greater traveller even than her hostess, she had been out of Europe, to Majorca, and Barbara had quite a corner in Umbrian hill-towns. Mrs. Prelude nonetheless retained a point of superiority; she had not gone, but been taken, abroad; and for all their independence, and strong-minded ways with foreign porters, both Miss Champney and Barbara in their heart of hearts knew that foreign travel was far jollier with a man.

So did Elizabeth a generation later.

2.

"Greece, my dear?" suggested Elizabeth. "A couple of months in Greece? Rather bliss?"

She wasn't in residence, at her women's college, she had her own flat in Bayswater. Which was just as well: Elizabeth stretching her long naked legs between the sheets of a three-quarters-size bed entwined limbs even longer, and hairy.

"In one sense," agreed Henry Alcott. "In one sense, I couldn't agree more, my wine-dark sea. A prick of masculine pride still arises."

"Has arisen."

"And will undoubtedly arise again, as soon as they switch that damned light off." (Elizabeth's flat unfortunately faced a small hotel struggling against discretion; the illuminated sign *ALOHA* went on and off like a would-be delinquent desperately signalling a magistrate. Elizabeth had observed its antiaphrodisiac effect before, but the flat was rent-controlled.) "What I mean, immediately," said Henry Alcott, "is that it's you who'd be paying the bills."

"And why not, now I've come into money?"

"Actually I read your dad's obituary in *The Times*," said Henry, sitting up and reaching for the glass of water he always put handy. "I've been wondering whether I mightn't do a Profile of him."

"You'll get no human touches from *me*," said Elizabeth.

"Not human, personal," corrected Henry, making the journalist's distinction. "It's quite extraordinary how little anyone knows about him, outside a conference room. I mean, how did he prepare those terrifically important speeches? Did he pace his study all night on relays of hot milk, or swig brandy in the bath?"

"Some would say you choose an unsuitable moment to try and pump me," observed Elizabeth.

"A really decent Profile, and I might be able to pay my own fare," pointed out Henry.

"Ethically, mightn't it be preferable to draw on Dad's cash rather than sell his braces? —But I'll tell you one thing about him," said Elizabeth, making a really brilliant leap at her object, "Father hated money to be inactive. Fort Worth gave him the willies. He'd have regarded your further education, my love, as a perfectly sensible investment."

In deference to her father's opinion Elizabeth so pressed the point, before dawn broke and Henry looked for his shoes he was in full agreement. —Fly to Athens first, they decided; then Delphi, then Rhodes.

3.

"So we can get married straight away," said William to his betrothed.

She was a lovely girl, as daughters of Oxford dons often are. Born to pick and choose, even if born plain they bloom. William's Alice (the Rev. C. L. Dodgson a friend of her grandmother's) had bloomed like a primrose—sleek yellow locks descendant from a centre-parting, smooth pale skin that tanned to biscuit without any intermediate stage of redness. Her eyes and eye-lashes and eye-brows were brown. However William had induced her to become engaged to him he still couldn't imagine, and lived in perpetual fear that she might suddenly meet someone handsomer, cleverer, richer, and change her mind.

"I'll have to talk to Daddy," said Alice.

William's expression of adoration instantly changed to one of ferocious dislike. He was used to these violent reversals of sentiment; after an hour in the company of his beloved he often felt as though he'd been ducked alternately into hot and cold water and then wrung out. It was one of the reasons he was so anxious to marry at once and get it over.

"You know perfectly well," William said furiously, "you've your daddy in your pocket. And if your mummy were alive you'd have her in the other. You're simply stalling me off, playing cat-and-mouse with me, and I'm damned if I'm going to stand it any longer."

It was the first time he had ever spoken so roughly to her. But he had the dutch courage of twenty thousand pounds in him.

"Don't bully me," said Alice plaintively. (Or interestedly? She cultivated a low, little-girl voice that gave nothing away. She even swore in a low, little-girl voice. Sometimes the trick made William feel faint with love, sometimes, as now, blind with rage. It was another version of the hot-and-cold, wrung-out formula.)

"I'm not bullying you. I am simply," snarled William, "putting the reasonable proposition that since we are allegedly engaged, and since I am now in a position to support a wife, we should dammit get married."

"But, darling, you're in *mourning*," reminded Alice.

"If you like, we'll have a black wedding."

"I'm making every allowance," said Alice, "but I hope you know you're being quite intolerable?"

The amorous tension between them was stretched almost to breaking-point; could indeed have found full relief only in a double bed. By a deliberate effort of will William put his intelligence into gear; with the result that he suddenly realized that he understood as little of what went on in his beloved's mind as if she'd been a mermaid or a Presbyterian. Did she really feel any thought of marrying or giving in marriage in the circumstances intolerable, or was she simply playing cat-and-mouse with him again? —As she suddenly turned away, was the brush of primrose-coloured hair against his cheek accidental, or deliberate? William hadn't a clue. He only knew it was like being flagellated with a feather . . .

He hadn't a clue, but he had an idea. His intelligence, as had notoriously been his father's, was evidently impartial. Having first issued a warning, it now came up with a spur.

"I'll tell you something about *my* father," said William. "Not my daddy," he added distastefully, "my father. He always wanted me to marry young. He often told me—"

Here William had to pause, since so far as he could recollect his parent had never conversed with him on any subject of importance whatever, let alone matrimony. But like Elizabeth he could improvise when needful.

"—that marrying my mother when they were both practically under-age was the whole basis of his career. If there's any filial duty *I* owe," said William loudly, "it's to get married at once and not be strung along for another year or so while you eye the new entry. In fact, either marry me or don't, next month."

The lock of hair brushed back; this time settled on his shoulder.

"And get rid of that damned jeep," ordered William.

"A girl still has to collect her bits and pieces," murmured Alice. "Could you make it September?"

4.

"Mother isn't going to like it," said Elizabeth.

"Mother likes Alice," argued William. "Mother dotes on her."

"Mother thinks Alice a very sweet girl," said Elizabeth. "Mother has a very innocent nature. She still isn't going to like your getting married within three months of Father's funeral."

"If it comes to that, she wouldn't like some of *your* extramural activities at any time."

"But she doesn't know about them," pointed out Elizabeth. "She hasn't the faintest suspicion."

"She has a very innocent nature," agreed William.

As he had ignored his sister's hit, so did she his.

"Whereas your wedding of course she must know about," continued Elizabeth. "She'll have to be there, looking reasonably festive. I do honestly think, William, you're being extraordinarily inconsiderate."

It occurred to William that his sister Elizabeth combined in a most remarkable way the characters of wanton and prig. (Or mermaid and Presbyterian; the equivalent of swearing in a low, little-girl voice.) Had all women such dual natures, wondered William nervously—tresses unbound both to flagellate and soothe? —Or even triple natures? Contemplating his sister Elizabeth, to all outward appearance the embodiment of cool intellect, he strongly suspected so; and was terrified, because if after knowing Elizabeth all his life he still didn't understand her, how after a mere two years could he tell whether Alice was marrying him for his money, or because he'd bullied her into it, or because she truly loved him?

He supposed he'd just have to find out afterwards.

"Without any intent to marry," said William deliberately, "how long was it after you met your latest that you jumped into bed with him? A couple of weeks?"

"I hope you know you're being quite insufferable," said Elizabeth.

"You and Alice are going to get on better than you think," said William. "I've yearned a couple of years, without so much as a furtive week-end to allay me. Now I've yearned long enough, and be damned to Father's funeral."

He paused. The impulse to annoy Elizabeth further got the upper hand.

"If it *was* Father's?" added William.

5.

Mrs. Prelude however accepted the news with surprising aplomb. William's reminder of how young she had married herself undoubtedly weighed with her; the period of her own engagement, she fondly recalled, had lasted but one month; poor Alice, who had waited two years!

"She wouldn't mind it being a *quiet* wedding?" asked Mrs. Prelude. "Of course white—and of course I'd come out of mourning—but really *quiet?*"

"Alice will agree to anything I suggest," promised William recklessly.

"I don't think you should ask Lydia to be bridesmaid."

"Alice won't want any bridesmaids."

"I wish I knew how your father would feel about it!" sighed Mrs. Prelude.

Panic seized William again. If his mother, who'd lived with his father half a lifetime, couldn't make even a shot at her husband's feeling about the marriage (admittedly in unusual circumstances) of their son, wasn't it possible that the masculine nature remained ever as impenetrable to the female understanding as the feminine to that of the male? And if so, into what emotional labyrinth of false clues and blind alleys was he rushing? Mightn't he as well rush down a railway track into the path of an express? But rush he had to. He couldn't help himself.

"What you mayn't know, Mother, is that Father always wanted me to marry young—just as he did. He said it was the whole basis of his success."

"Did he really?" asked Mrs. Prelude wistfully.

"Only he wanted me to stand on my own feet first, and the trouble was he knew absolutely nothing about the antique-trade. He was a wizard at the new franc, but he hadn't a clue what a Louis Fifteenth commode would fetch at Sotheby's. He simply couldn't grasp that all I needed was a bit of capital. Perhaps now he does," said William reverently, "and in any case, Mother, the one thing I am certain of is that now I *can* stand on my own feet, he'd want me to marry Alice straight away."

The sophistry which Elizabeth would have pounced on at once passed over Mrs. Prelude's head. Besides, she was always easily swayed by anyone she loved.

"Then if you're really sure, dear, write and put poor Alice's mind at rest at once," said Mrs. Prelude. —"Poor Elizabeth!" she added, to herself at least with perfect relevance. "Going off to Greece all alone!"

Fresh from scrapping with Elizabeth as he was, William was still loyal to his generation.

"Elizabeth has her career, Mother. Father often said how proud he was of her."

"Your father seems to have talked to you children far more than he ever did to me!" sighed Mrs. Prelude. "You must tell me everything you remember."

6.

It was quite surprising how much they remembered. Elizabeth, down for the week-end, and alerted by her brother, was particularly fertile in sympathetic anecdotes. "Don't you remember how pleased and proud he was, Mother," prompted Elizabeth, "when I made my first speech at the Union?" "I thought we were in Holland," said Mrs. Prelude. "Yes, but how pleased and proud he was to hear about it afterwards!" said Elizabeth hastily. "Don't you remember?"

Mrs. Prelude actually didn't. What she chiefly remembered was that Arthur's inhaling-apparatus had gone wrong. Nor could she honestly say she recalled her husband greeting Alice with a kiss, as William said he did; the pictures were so pretty, however, Mrs. Prelude willingly, gratefully, accepted them. —Delving further back, into memories of childhood, William and Elizabeth recalled gay bonfires on Guy Fawkes night made even gayer by their father's presence. Mrs. Prelude had always thought the gardener was simply burning rubbish, and that why Arthur went out was to stop him because of the sparks. It was a true pleasure to her to know that at heart he had been such a family man.

"We should have lied to Mother sooner," said Elizabeth.

"How could we, while Father was still alive?" countered William.

"Perhaps what we're pretending now was really the truth," said Elizabeth. "Perhaps when he came out to stop the bonfire he was secretly hoping we'd rush towards him with welcoming cries."

"Perhaps he really did kiss Alice."

"You'd better remind her," said Elizabeth.

7.

"But he didn't," protested Alice. (Over a table at the Ritz: if she drove her jeep all the way to London just for lunch, the Ritz was where she intended to be lunched. William knew of several more exciting also less expensive venues round about Soho, but as Alice pointed out, a girl after having been so scared by horrible great lorries didn't want excitement: just peace in the Ritz.) "He didn't," repeated Alice. "I was totally astonished. I mean, most old men simply jump at the chance. I keep a special hanky to wipe their drooling whiskers."

"Heartless brat," said William—thus lightly concealing, or so he hoped, a pang of jealousy at once ridiculous, unworthy, and sharp as a serpent's tooth. "You will still, to please my mother, remember that Dad saluted you with a kiss."

To his surprise, Alice appeared to search her memory.

"Of course I was terribly nervous—I mean, meeting your father for the first time. I expect I was too nervous to remember anything."

William, about to point out that she'd just perfectly recollected her astonishment at the lack of an embrace, perceived that he had better let her take her own line. Evidently Alice, unlike himself and Elizabeth, preferred the deviousness of self-deception to a straight lie. What didn't occur to him was that Arthur Prelude's rebuff—not a drool drooled, Alice's hanky at the ready merely to put up again—was something Alice genuinely wished hadn't happened. It spoiled her record.

"Did you *see* him kiss me?" asked Alice hopefully.

"On both cheeks," affirmed William. "Then he was so overcome he had to take the next train to town."

—Again to his surprise, Alice nodded seriously. Her lovely face grew abstracted. William took the opportunity to order melon before she demanded caviare.

"It seems so tragic that was the only time we ever met," sighed Alice, "when he was such an old sweetie-pie . . ."

4

MRS. PRELUDE'S RECOVERY was rapid. As week succeeded week the atmosphere in the house at Chesham Bois from being cosy became almost gay: why move to Hove at all, with Buckinghamshire so convenient to the comings and goings of William and Elizabeth, and the Wilfreds only ten miles off, and dear Alice often staying with friends nearby? Mrs. Prelude felt well content where she was; and if she sometimes woke in the hours after midnight from a dream in which her Arthur had returned to her—if she sometimes, in those small hours, sat up in one half of a double bed and asked herself afresh whether she'd really been *sure*—by morning she was always quite happy and rational again. Indeed these recurrent dreams were rather a comfort to Mrs. Prelude, who had often heard of people living on in people's thoughts but whose own waking thoughts were increasingly occupied by the prospects of a Liberal candidate at Tring or a poodle bitch at Cruft's. Her dreams, as it were, took over; and with Arthur really so alive in them, she felt cosiness (and even gaiety) excusable.

"Dear Arthur! He'd always want it to be a *happy* house,"

explained Mrs. Prelude to Harriet and Barbara, "just as it was when he was still with us . . ."

"Actually I never thought he spent much time at home at all," said Miss Champney.

"How could he?" returned Mrs. Prelude, "when he was so terribly in demand? Even when Elizabeth made her first speech at the Union he had to be in Holland. But how pleased and proud he was to hear about it afterwards! It was a side of him few people knew."

"It was a side of him no one knew," rather apologized Miss Champney.

"Outside his family," agreed Mrs. Prelude. "To be alone with his family was Arthur's one joy."

Miss Hume and Miss Champney accepted the revelation with pleasure. It explained, for instance, Arthur's barely concealed impatience to see them leave after a mere week-end: he wanted to be alone with his family. More enviable than ever appeared Mrs. Prelude, foreign travel but an interlude in domestic bliss; her friends never tired of hearing the details—which in truth interested them far more, though neither would have admitted it, than any accounts of international conferences. Barbara's favourite bit was about Alice being kissed; Miss Champney's (she herself having enrolled at the L.S.E. in the teeth of paternal opposition), the delight shown in Elizabeth's Oxford success. "You say he gave her a gold wrist-watch?" recapped Miss Champney. —Mrs. Prelude didn't exactly remember having said so, but she might well have done: certainly Elizabeth possessed and wore a gold wrist-watch. (Actually inscribed on the back, *What a wench!*—but her mother had never seen the back.) "Arthur liked to give all his children pleasure," said Mrs. Prelude tenderly, "but I believe it was their long, serious talks with him they really enjoyed most."

Her friends could well believe it. This was perhaps the bit they liked best of all.

"What an advantage it must have been to them!" sighed Barbara once. "I scarcely remember my father talking to me at all. Did yours, dear?"

"Only to tell me I'd no brains worth educating," said Miss Champney bitterly.

"I suppose it doesn't take much brains to clip a poodle," said modest Miss Hume, "but mine didn't think me capable even of that. The pom-poms still take a good deal of concentration; some owners think, even artistry."

"I misjudged him," said Harriet frankly. "I always of course immensely respected his intellect, but I never realized how, well, warm he was."

"Nor I," regretted Barbara, "while he was still alive." She paused. "Did *you* send a wreath, dear? I'm afraid I didn't."

"No," said Miss Champney. "I'm afraid I didn't either."

"Then don't you think we might? I mean, even if it's a bit late it can still be put on . . ."

Thus on top of the decaying mounded tributes from Holland, Sweden, West Germany, Saudi Arabia, Les Banques Industrielles de l'Indo-Chine and Portugal's Banco Maritime y do Nova Zembla, a simpler garland found place. —The card actually one of Miss Hume's tradecards: but with the rubric *Poodle-clipping a Speciality* crossed out there was plenty of room for Miss Champney's name as well, also the brief inscription *Out of strength came forth sweetness.*

2.

"I must say I never thought she'd take it so well," observed Mrs. Wilfred, driving back with her husband from a second visit of condolence. —Their first, immediate, pre-funeral visit had found Mrs. Prelude so distressingly blanched and almost speechless, only a certain guilt about their absence from that funeral had impelled them to drive over again within the next weeks. "I mean," added Mrs. Wilfred, "she was always so dependent on Arthur . . ."

"She has two adult children to support her," observed Wilfred Prelude, deliberately changing gear. He drove not so much expertly as doggedly: even at a steady forty miles per hour the Rover was difficult to overtake. So had his brother, metaphorically, held the crown of the road, doggedly refusing to be overtaken by Renault or Volkswagen. —An Opel behind hooted without effect.

"Did *you* ever realize he was such a family man?" asked Mrs. Wilfred presently.

"My late lamented brother," responded Wilfred Prelude, "so far as I know never had a thought in his head outside economics."

"Perhaps you didn't know him very well, darling."

Necessarily halting before traffic-lights, Wilfred Prelude was able to turn and scrutinize his wife's profile. —He didn't often look at her, as Mrs. Wilfred was well aware.

Her nose, shaped rather like a puffin's beak, but still in its way handsome, her carefully rouged mouth and carefully plucked eyebrows, were too familiar. What he now saw surprised him: down the carefully rouged cheek a tear trickled.

"Naturally I knew him," said Wilfred Prelude. "I felt the greatest respect for him. He had by all accounts one of the best brains in Europe."

The tribute was both sincere and unenvious; Wilfred Prelude's own intellect, though less gigantic than his elder brother's, had sufficed to make him so highly salaried an industrial consultant he could afford a bigger house and bigger car, also a butler. It wasn't he, it had been his wife, who felt Arthur might have remembered them in his will; but she'd got over it, so why was she crying now?

"We never had a bonfire-night for Toby," sighed Mrs. Wilfred.

"If Toby had wanted a bonfire," pointed out Toby's father reasonably, "he'd have suggested it."

"Yes, darling; but it was Arthur who suggested theirs; I've just been hearing. That's why the children enjoyed it so . . . I believe he was much more affectionate than we realized," said Mrs. Wilfred, "only too reserved to show it. Perhaps he wished *we'd* shown more affection to *him*; I rather reproach myself."

She was a worldly woman; a woman Elizabeth steadily disliked for her material complacency in a big house, a big car, an Italian butler. No more than her husband his brother had Mrs. Wilfred ever envied her sister-in-law; she too thoroughly preferred under-floor heating throughout to any amount of reflected celebrity. Now, however, as a fresh tear trickled, she found herself envying.

3.

"Sweetie-pie?" mused Professor Harvill. "Arthur Prelude?"

"You hardly met him," said Alice, answering her parent's tone more than his words. "He was a lamb."

"Actually only twice," said Professor Harvill, who prided himself on an un-donnish memory for the stray facts of life. "Once in connection with an appeal to endow a scholarship in memory of Maynard Keynes, once at an equally interested luncheon in aid of the Liberal Party Fighting Fund. On neither occasion did he subscribe."

"Did you either, Daddy?"

"Certainly not," said Professor Harvill. "I thought all the better of him for it."

"What I was working up to, to sort of *prepare* you," said Alice, "is why William has such a terrific *loyalty* it's making him absolutely *inconsiderate*. He says his father—"

"Arthur Prelude?" checked Professor Harvill. "William Prelude?"

"Darling, haven't I been engaged to him for *years?*" reminded Alice.

"You've been getting engaged ever since you were sixteen," reminded her parent in turn. —It was true; and Professor Harvill had long washed his hands of Alice's under-age fiancés, amongst whom William (remembered only from tutorials) in fact still figured to him. Even more decidedly, ever since Alice got engaged to the son of a

Greek shipping-owner, had her father avoided any encounter with potential relatives-in-law. He'd rather looked forward to meeting a modern Greek, to discuss certain switches of accent and diphthongs; the scantily draped offer of a thousand pounds to call Alice off had sent Professor Harvill back from the Ritz to the Athenaeum both affronted and perturbed. Mr. Xerxes, rather admiringly, suspected him of holding out for more, but Madame, with greater perception, had a heart-attack, and young Cyril after being hastily called to her side found himself on the way home to Athens. Oxford saw him no more; Alice wept for a few days, her father hoped from blighted affection, then the episode was closed, but it was one Professor Harvill never forgot. It taught him to stay strictly on the side-lines. Thus he had paid scant heed to any mention of William, and was now genuinely astonished to realize how long ago those tutorials had been. —Before Alice could begin to cry (as she usually did at any reference to past loves), her parent had performed a rough calculation.

"He's over twenty-one?"

Alice had indeed a tear in her eye, but found it still appropriate.

"Twenty-five, darling. That's why again," grieved Alice. "He says his father always wanted him to marry young because he did himself and it was the whole basis of his career. I'm terribly sorry, Daddy—"

"If to that agreeable woman with him at the luncheon," put in Professor Harvill, quite warmly, "I dare say he was right. I was struck at the time by her quickness in procuring him grapefruit instead of the lobster cocktail. It seems he had an allergy to shellfish."

Like William and Elizabeth on the day of the funeral, Alice felt lobster (in any form) a jarring note. She allowed a few seconds to pass before she gently took her parent's hand and spoke again.

"What I'm trying to tell you, Daddy darling, is that William wants us to get married quite *soon* . . ."

Professor Harvill's eye brightened.

"How soon?"

"September," confessed Alice. "He says it's what his father would have wanted . . ."

Professor Harvill paused. It didn't for a moment occur to him to exclaim that surely no filial piety was needed to explain William's impatience. Alice was too like her mother for him to appreciate her looks; the havoc she played with a tutorial merely by putting her head round the door aroused in his academic mind a sympathy with the Spartans exposing female offspring on a hillside. Professor Harvill felt sorry for William as for one misled by filial piety. Arthur Prelude had undoubtedly good grounds for his advice ("Without even offending the waiter!" recalled Professor Harvill, in admiring parenthesis), but reflecting upon his own early marriage he could only pause. The mother of Alice (though death softens all things) had been a mistake: deceptively, softly pretty, the late Mrs. Harvill had turned out demanding, extravagant, self-centred and irrational: Professor Harvill's much-admired Spartan demeanour on the occasion of her early demise in fact came easily to him. The prospect of losing his daughter as well— not by death either; after all she was only twenty, it might have looked as if her chest had been neglected—filled him with thanksgiving. He compassionated William, he felt

Arthur Prelude seriously to blame, but neither emotion weighed a feather against his feelings towards Alice. He didn't pause long.

"God bless you, my child," said Professor Harvill briskly. "Just see the date's in my diary and I'll be there to give you away."

4.

As not infrequently at High Table when the Reader in English was present, the talk veered towards American infiltration speech-wise. It was his hobby-horse. His colleagues of other schools riding other hobbies, only the Chaplain's reminder that Chaucer-wise "*I guess*" was old hat fell pat and familiar as a response at matins.

"*Babe*, also," agreed the Reader, "has been one might say returned to us; if with an extension of reference to any personable young female. *Honey* too one could probably trace, if not *honey-bun*. But endearment-wise our cousins undoubtedly show imagination."

"Sweetie-pie," offered Professor Harvill.

The Master regarded him with raised eye-brows. In general opinion, to which Alice's father had always hitherto subscribed, the best way of throwing any other chap's hobby-horse was to present a metaphorical ha-ha—i.e., a concealed sunken ditch: translated speech-wise into dead silence—and let it flounder therein. Very rarely did the Master (and then only if guests were present) feel forced to put a pistol to the poor brute's head; but that Professor

Harvill was actually helping it onto its legs again naturally astonished him.

"Not at all," said Professor Harvill swiftly. (He and the Master had dined together more years than either could count.) "Why the phrase came into my mind was actually in connection with Arthur Prelude. You remember him, Master, at that Liberal luncheon?"

"Certainly," said the Master. "You surprise me."

"He didn't subscribe," put in the Chaplain, who had.

"The majority showed equal sense; but at least we had sufficient courtesy not to give our reasons. Prelude's exposition of the Liberals' irretrievable financial bankruptcy (*per capita* came into it, one recalls: also some simile about rattling buttons in a collecting-box) may have been brilliant, and possibly well intentioned; but hardly a sweetmeat?"

"It seems one had to know him in his family," said Professor Harvill. "My daughter Alice is actually engaged to his son. —What occured to me, Master, is that a letter of condolence, University-wise, might not come amiss. He was obviously in line for an honorary degree of some sort, and I believe she'd appreciate it."

"Your daughter Alice?" enquired the Reader in English sceptically.

"His wife," corrected Professor Harvill. "She sat next to you, Master."

"That amiable woman Mrs. Prelude?" enquired the Master. "You know it as a fact?"

"Considering my daughter is about to marry her son, yes, Master."

"One certainly thinks better of him," said the Master.

"All the same, University-wise, I wouldn't care to put it up. Economics still hasn't forgotten how he bashed into Maynard Keynes. (Another brilliant speech: how rarely tact and brilliance join!) But if you care to write yourself, my dear fellow, I shall be happy to be associated with any appropriate sentiment. —Also examine your motives," said the Master. "Why the deuce shouldn't you write to her?"

Why not indeed? The truth was that Professor Harvill still hadn't quite taken in the idea of any natural social connection, so to speak, between himself and Arthur Prelude's widow. He hadn't even fully taken in the idea of her widowhood. Now, examining, as the Master bade him, his motives, he discovered them to be amazingly forward. He was as surprised as if looking at himself in the mirror while shaving he had suddenly perceived his whiskers not grey but mid-brown again.

"One might even call?" reflected Professor Harvill.

More from habit than religious faith he kept beside his bed, along with whatever detective-story he happened to be reading, the Book of Common Prayer. Idly fluttering its pages that night he chanced upon the table of Kindred and Affinity. There didn't seem to be anything about one's daughter's mother-in-law.

5.

"How everyone *appreciated* Arthur!" exclaimed Mrs. Prelude, with tender pride. "The Master's asked Professor Harvill to write specially to send his sympathy . . ."

(So indeed had Professor Harvill a trifle disingenuously

opened: *The Master asks me to convey to you;* still as it were uncertain of the colour of his whiskers.)

"Which Master?" asked Miss Hume suspiciously. "I didn't know Arthur hunted?"

"Not of Fox-hounds, College," corrected Miss Champney. "Try not to be such a fool, dear."

"*His brilliant intellect,*" re-read Mrs. Prelude, "*is his country's and so I am told probably the Common Market's loss: the amiable qualities displayed in intimacy I dare say only his family can adequately mourn . . .* It's so wonderful how Arthur's loveableness shone through."

"Indeed it did," said Miss Hume. "That's why I was so surprised to think he hunted. He would have been more likely to belong to the Anti-Blood-Sports League."

"How does it go on?" asked Miss Champney.

"Oh, just something about coming to call," said Mrs. Prelude carelessly. "I expect about the wedding. Poor man, how he must wish Alice's mother still alive!"

There was a second letter for Mrs. Prelude that morning, air-mail, with a Greek stamp. Corinna van Hoyt's sympathy, affection and apologies for delay in writing filled three pages—admittedly she scrawled barely four words to a line—and ended, rather casually, with the news that she was getting a divorce.

Mrs. Prelude was so shocked and distressed, she felt glad there was no address to write back to. She could hardly have thought what to say, fond as she was of both the van Hoyts. Of course Corinna was more specially her friend; but how kind and considerate, at any short encounter, Corinna's husband! Mrs. Prelude recalled his more than once coming up for a little chat at an airport or on a railway platform. She didn't want to blame Corinna—Mrs. Prelude never wanted to blame anyone—but her sympathies were at least divided, and not to have to define them in writing was a true relief.

For a woman so accustomed to foreign travel she appeared to be missing it surprisingly little, for when her friends suggested a joint scamper to the Canaries she damped the plan at once. This wasn't however because she felt her travelling days over—she in fact felt younger than for years—nor even because she rightly foresaw that the bulk of expense would fall upon herself, but simply because she couldn't envisage travelling anywhere without a man. Careful of her spinster-friends' susceptibilities, what Mrs. Prelude told, reminded Barbara and Harriet, was that Lydia was due home for the holidays.

6.

Lydia came home looking like a ghost. There was no colour in her cheeks, she had rings under her eyes; her long ponytail of black hair, in need of trimming, drooped like a mourning veil. She looked less as though she'd come to holiday in that happy house than to haunt it.

"Poor wee one!" murmured Miss Hume sympathetically. "The youngest, and I expect her father's pet?"

"Arthur never made favourites," said Mrs. Prelude—loyal however worried; embracing Lydia had been like hugging a parcel of chicken-bones. "Still the youngest *is* always the youngest . . . I only made her go back to school because William and Elizabeth absolutely insisted."

"She would have been better at your side," said Miss Champney. "I've never seen a child so haggard."

"We must have everything she likes best to eat," said Mrs. Prelude. "Like fried chicken . . ."

Miss Hume and Miss Champney were fond of fried chicken themselves. A series of meals based on this dish, preceded now by a lobster cocktail, now by an avocado pear (Lydia's other favourite foods), almost consoled them for not going to the Canaries. They in fact tucked in far more whole-heartedly than did Lydia.

"A little more, darling?" pressed Mrs. Prelude.

"No thank you, Mother," said Lydia politely.

She looked haggard as a young witch: and when one midnight shortly after her return an owl hooted in the orchard, pulled a coat over her pyjamas and like a witch ran out to greet her familiar spirit.

5

TOBY HAD PROPPED his bicycle against an apple-tree. —It was a machine in the last stages of decrepitude: vintage. He himself wore vintage knickerbockers, orange skiing jacket, and espadrilles. Owing to his extreme handsomeness, however, and in the moonlight, there was somehow projected the image of young knight and tethered steed.

"I got your letter," said Toby. "It wasn't very enlightening."

"I couldn't be," said Lydia, "in case it fell into other hands. But thank goodness you've come!"

"Of course I came. —I'm sorry I wasn't at Uncle Arthur's funeral," added Toby politely. "I still think my people should have been; though actually I was able to pass off Mamma's hat as a vicarious floral tribute. Was it very harrowing?"

"Not the funeral," said Lydia. "Afterwards. That's what I couldn't write about." She paused. What she had to reveal was so tremendous, its consequences were going to be so glorious, astonishing and far-reaching, when it came to the point of utterance she almost dried up. It was the

[49]

biggest line of her life. "Oh, Toby," said Lydia, "it *wasn't* Father's funeral!"

2.

"Elizabeth and William think Mother's just imagined everything," explained Lydia, some minutes later. "But William wants to get married to Alice—"

"He must be insane," said Toby.

"I didn't know you knew her?" said Lydia, momentarily diverted.

"Her dad coached me in Latin. Itsy-bitsy popsy-totsy, also teeny-weeny kitty-kitty."

"Insane," sighed Lydia. "And Elizabeth wants to go to Greece, and I think, and I think William thinks, she's taking some awful gigolo with her. Father'd never have stumped up for either of them; so they were both predisposed. I mean, what evidence have they, to think Father's dead?"

Toby broke off an apple-twig and chewed on it.

"Well, you might say your mother's," he pointed out. "Then there's the air-line; you can bet the air-line was searching for survivors like blazes, if only to keep the death-roll down. If Uncle Arthur's still alive, what's become of him? V.I.P.s don't just disappear."

"Father could," said Lydia. "He never *looked* like a V.I.P. Even in photographs while he was making a speech there had to be an arrow pointed at him. —He was flung out and lost his memory," said Lydia rapidly, "and wandered away into the mountains and was taken in by simple peasants the air-line never thought of asking."

3.

Down streamed the moonlight (notoriously destructive of rationality), washing away the last of Toby's doubts. His imagination leaping to meet his cousin's—

"In which case," said Toby grimly, "he's probably hoeing away for dear life . . ."

Lydia shuddered. "Sleeping in an outhouse like a poor old watch-dog . . ."

"Let's only hope they give him enough to eat."

"How Elizabeth and William *can!*" cried Lydia passionately. "Mother's different, I truly believe Mother's forgotten everything she told us. But Elizabeth and William must remember, and how they can leave Father starving in a shed for the sake of a measly twenty thousand apiece is simply too macabre."

"I believe we all get mercenary with age," said wise Toby. "My own mamma was quite sick at being left out."

Dappled by moonlight falling between apple-boughs, the two young faces turned to each other in common repudiation of adult corruptness.

"It makes one ashamed of the human race," said Lydia severely. "But that's obviously why the others won't do anything and it's up to us."

The cousins never had need for many words with each other. They had been too long in league.

"To go and look for him?" said Toby at once.

[51]

"To go and find him. I've an absolute instinct," said Lydia. "I know we'll find him."

"It means getting to France first."

"Everyone's always going to France. Especially in the summer holidays. Whole crocodiles of schoolchildren go. The whole of our Upper Fourth's going."

"But with a free hand," said Toby, "which is just what our loving families won't want to give us—unless of course we tell why?"

"Definitely not," said Lydia. "It would be too cruel, to raise Mother's hopes and then leave her in suspense. Besides, William and Elizabeth would stop us."

"I agree with you," said Toby. "Until we can actually send a wire the less said the better. —You've still got something with that crocodile."

Lydia waited respectfully while he chewed again. Though she would have scouted the charge as indignantly as that of avarice, she had inherited her mother's esteem for the male intellect.

"Youth Clubs," pronounced Toby at last. "On bikes. Have you got one?"

"Brand-new," said Lydia distastefully. "Mother gave it me—can you imagine!—for my last birthday. Why bikes?"

"To search on, in the mountains. We'll take our bikes by train as near as we can to where the crash was—"

"Chambérieu," supplied Lydia.

"—and start from there searching yard by yard."

Only a few minutes more of colloquy ensued—tremendously important, wonderfully exciting—before he leapt on his own machine (or knightly steed) and pedalled off.

4.

"But I thought you loathed Youth Clubs!" exclaimed Mrs. Wilfred.

"Cycling's still the best way of seeing a country," said Toby, "and they work out the routes jolly well. And as Lydia's going—"

"Lydia is?"

"It's a Mixed Youth Cycling Club," explained Toby.

His mother reflected a moment. She knew the cousins affectionate, but rightly believed them not dangerously so. In fact she thought Lydia's company no bad thing, for so handsome a youth on the loose. What influenced her even more was the thought of dear old Arthur—so affectionate, so dumbly seeking to strengthen family ties; and though the Youth Club's charge for a fortnight's tour struck her as high, she not unwillingly bought Toby travellers' cheques for forty pounds.

Toby had aimed at fifty; but when Mrs. Wilfred said she'd have to speak to his father, settled for forty. In this instance, however, perhaps a chance might have been taken; to Toby's astonishment, on the eve of his departure Wilfred Prelude spontaneously came across with an extra tenner.

5.

"I must say it's nice to know you were really *pleased* with your bicycle," said Mrs. Prelude. "I was afraid you weren't."

"Darling, I'm mad about it," said Lydia.

Though it was a pleasure to see the child looking so much brighter, Mrs. Prelude hesitated.

"I'm still not sure I quite like the idea, darling: cycling all about France with perfect strangers."

"Toby's going," said Lydia. "It was Toby," she added truthfully, "who suggested it."

Mrs. Prelude no more than her sister-in-law suspected any over-warm attachment; rather (again like her sister-in-law), welcomed a cousinly chaperonage.

"That does make a difference," admitted Mrs. Prelude, "if you'll have Toby to look after you . . ."

Lydia got a hundred. Mrs. Prelude, thanks to Arthur, was used to so far larger figures—loans of fifty thousand here, a couple of million there—a hundred pounds struck her as just a nice little round sum.

6.

Their finances thus assured, Toby and Lydia before they set out had still to suffer a good deal of advice from their elders and betters rather haphazardly assembled at Sunday lunch. —Elizabeth was there to collect a suitcase, William to pick up *Chefs d'oeuvre du Mobilier Français*, Mrs. Wilfred because Toby was; but not Harriet or Barbara, who either from tact or because Mrs. Prelude suggested it, had taken a picnic.

"For heaven's sake don't lose your passports," warned Elizabeth.

"Or get your bicycles stolen," warned William.

"Or your pockets picked, darlings," said Mrs. Wilfred, who had once lost a purse in Notre Dame.

"And don't drink too much red wine," added Elizabeth.

"Steer clear of con-men," added William.

"Also *louche* parties," added Elizabeth.

"Good gracious, you'd think the children were going quite by themselves," exclaimed Mrs. Prelude, "instead of with a Youth Club! —And you're just off to the Lakes," she checked, to Mrs. Wilfred, "and Elizabeth to Greece, so why don't we all meet here for lunch again in two weeks' time and tell each other everything that's happened?"

All agreed that this was a very nice idea.

7.

"I thought you said Greece for a couple of months?" observed William to Elizabeth before they separated.

"A fortnight is mother's Platonic idea of a summer holiday," said Elizabeth. "Don't you remember, when we were little, and before Father was in the money, how she used to scrape all year to take us for a fortnight to the sea every August? When the time comes I shall just send a wire."

"Signed, *love, Elizabeth and Alistair?*"

"Henry," corrected Elizabeth.

"I see I'm one behind," said William. "At least."

"I'm sure you're quite attractive yourself," said Elizabeth, "only you're so fixated on Alice."

"Alice and I," said William, "have reached a perfect understanding. The wedding's on September the sixteenth.

[55]

Is your Alistair—sorry, Henry—sufficiently fixated to fix a date?"

"But I have no wish for him to," said Elizabeth. "We're just having a short sybaritic trip to Greece together . . ."

With unusual forbearance (his own prospects so happy) William didn't ask who'd be paying, though he guessed. In all families siblings know much more about each other than their parents do; Elizabeth's extramural activities might be a closed book to Mrs. Prelude, but Lydia at least winded them, while William was sufficiently informed to know that his elder sister's swains regularly presented two common characteristics: high intelligence and low bank-balance. As gentlemen prefer blondes, so Elizabeth seemed to prefer brilliant non-starters. William often wondered why, and had come to the brotherly conclusion that it was from bossiness. Elizabeth couldn't stomach a fool, but no more could she stomach taking a second place, and liked her own superiority of attainment to be undisputed. At least such was William's opinion.

8.

"I've promised we'll lunch practically the day we get back," reported Mrs. Wilfred to her husband. "Toby's dropping Lydia on the way home, and it seems rather a nice opportunity for us all to get together."

She was hardly surprised by Wilfred Prelude's ready agreement to visit his sister-in-law thrice within as many months; only felt a little sad because she couldn't in honesty attribute it to any burgeoning of family affection.

Wilfred Prelude took holidays solely on principle, as a preventive against ulcers; driving about the Lake District in a Rover at about forty miles per hour relaxed him. A fortnight was still as much as he could stand; actually the second week of this annual tour found him telephoning back each evening in case any captain of industry had been trying to make contact with him—in which event gladly he turned the Rover homewards. His particular dislike was having no specific date by which his return was absolutely necessary, so that not to take an extra day or two, if his wife, for example, wished to visit Coventry Cathedral, couldn't be justified. Sadly but percipiently, Mrs. Wilfred recognized her husband equating lunch at Chesham Bois with a board-meeting . . .

Then she was as surprised as Toby had been at his extra tenner.

"We might bring her back some little souvenir," offered Wilfred Prelude. "Of spar, perhaps; I remember seeing miniature obelisks." He paused. "When we were boys, Arthur and I, we had quite a fad for minerals. He used to take me to the National Geological."

"Two little boys in knickerbockers?" prompted Mrs. Wilfred. "One just big enough to take care of the other?"

"Certainly it was always Arthur who handled the bus-money," acknowledged Wilfred Prelude, "and somehow always produced a penny over to buy me a penny-bun."
—Young Wilfred had in fact been almost walked off his young legs to save a twopenny-stage, so young Arthur was still threepence up, but memory (into which the adult Wilfred so rarely dipped) was kind. "He must have been

an affectionate little fellow; I dare say you're right about him."

Thus even Arthur Prelude's brother came to subscribe to the new image of him (dead), just as the Master had come to subscribe to it, and Mrs. Wilfred, and Alice, and Professor Harvill, and Miss Hume and Miss Champney, and of course Mrs. Prelude herself. Dead, Arthur Prelude's domestic virtues outshone even his financial-wise ones. A follow-up letter from Professor Harvill (still as it were uncertain of the colour of his whiskers) quoted from Burns the bit about a happy fireside clime; Mrs. Prelude, tenderly paper-clipping it to his first, was gratified but unsurprised. She still thought the children might like to see it—especially Lydia.

6

WHY TOBY AND LYDIA, who according to plan should have entrained straight for Chambérieu on the borders of Switzerland and Haute Savoie, found themselves cycling along a *route nationale* in the Limousin, was because (as all children know, only they'd forgotten) if you tell a lie it is likely to come true. In brief, they encountered a Youth Club. Or if not precisely a Youth Club, even worse. In brief, the Chambérieu train was lively with almost the entire Upper Fourth from Lydia's own school in charge of the games-mistress. She spotted Lydia at once.

"Prelude!" exclaimed the games-mistress delightedly. "Lydia Prelude! I never knew one of our *seniors* had put down!"

"Actually I didn't—" began Lydia.

"Never mind!" beamed the games-mistress. "There's always an extra bed at a hostel! —Who's the lad?"

"M' cousin," said Lydia. —It was a trick she'd picked up from Toby's way of saying m' tutor. Upon the games-mistress, however, such fine shadings of the English language, with all they implied, were totally lost. Regarding a Captain of Boats less admiringly than indulgently—

"So long as he's *related*," exclaimed the games-mistress, "why not? We'll find *him* a bed with the Boo Scoots!"

So Lydia and Toby got out at the next stop. Obviously there was no alternative. Furtively they hauled their cycles from the luggage-van, furtively watched the train draw out, then bought themselves a hard-boiled egg apiece at the station buffet.

"We've only to catch the next," said Toby.

"Here?" asked Lydia.

Toby consulted the time-table. (He had a time-table, he had a map: carefully stowed along with their passports and money in the inside pocket of his skiing jacket. He was as much in charge as Arthur Prelude had always been in charge. It was he who'd thoughtfully cashed their travellers' cheques at once, lest their search took them into wilds where banks were unknown.)

"Actually from here there isn't another till tomorrow morning. But if we bike about five miles back down the line we can pick up the nineteen-fifty from Villeneuve-le-Duc."

So another lie came true; far sooner than they expected they were seeing the country.

2.

"I'd still see more without a rucksack," complained Lydia, pedalling between rows of poplars. "It makes me wobble."

They both had rucksacks, containing spare shoes, changes of underwear, tooth-paste and tooth-brushes, soap and face-flannels. They could hardly have travelled lighter, but with rucksacks strapped onto the carriers of their bikes behind, they still, as Lydia said, wobbled.

"Actually there isn't much to see yet," said Toby. "It's hardly Constable country."

"Actually I don't think it has anything on Bucks," panted Lydia. "What's a *jubé?*"

So the sign at the crossroads suddenly indicated: *Eglise St. Emilien, beau jubé.*

"Roodscreen," said Toby knowledgeably. He knew everything.

"Anyway we can sit down while we look at it," said Lydia. "We can't have much more than a mile to go."

So they turned and pedalled up a lane, and propped their bicycles outside a churchyard, and Lydia with her mother's international good manners pulled a scarf from her jeans pocket to tie round her head.

3.

The *beau jubé* was so huge, it almost filled the small edifice dedicated to St. Emilien: in the dim religious light obscured both choir and altar. There were a great many figures carved upon it, including two that looked like the Virgin and a Roman soldier: the rest, in the dim religious light, anonymous. It was still wonderfully impressive. Before the cousins approached nearer—

"I know you're an agnostic," said Lydia, "but would you mind if I lit a candle?"

Toby liberally bade her go ahead. He himself was touched to solemnity by the *beau jubé.* He knelt. Lydia came and knelt beside him. There was no one else in the little church. Toby courteously bowed his head; so did Lydia, and prayed.

"O Lord," prayed Lydia, "let me find my father . . ."

At that moment, as not infrequently happens just before sunset, a last spectacular ray suddenly penetrated. Through the west window behind them light so flooded, the whole *jubé* started to life. The Virgin leaned forth in blessing, the Roman soldier, and even Pontius Pilate (revealed low down on the left), seemed to signal encouragement. Lydia felt like Joan of Arc hearing voices in the bells.

4.

In Buckinghamshire at just about the same time Mrs. Prelude was receiving a visit of condolence not from Professor Harvill, but from Mr. van Hoyt. She felt extremely flattered, and showed it, that he'd squeezed her in between Zürich and Amsterdam.

"To come all this way just for an hour!" murmured Mrs. Prelude. "But then Arthur really was, wasn't he, in his way, great?"

"The greatest," said Mr. van Hoyt solemnly.

He didn't fail to notice how swiftly, instinctively, she transferred the compliment from herself to her husband. It was a sort of womanly modesty Mr. van Hoyt found both becoming and unusual. As for Mrs. Prelude, she was additionally gratified to hear Arthur's praises from one who truly knew how to value him—that is, in his public character: it was naturally impossible for anyone who'd met him only at conferences to know about the bonfires and kissing Alice. Eagerly Mrs. Prelude listened to Mr. van Hoyt's judicious summing of Arthur's expertise, experience, and special flair. He gave illustrations—the background, for example (including half-a-year's homework and last statistics digested overnight), to that famous slaughter of the French. It was as good as a lecture; if Mrs. Prelude had had paper and pencil handy, she'd have been drawing rabbits. In short, nothing could have distracted her attention for a single instant except the knowledge that Corinna was seeking a divorce. It was naturally the first thought to enter Mrs. Prelude's mind the moment Mr. van Hoyt walked in, and she couldn't get it out again.

So far, he had made no mention of Corinna. No doubt the subject was too painful, the wound still too fresh? Yet Mr. van Hoyt didn't look wounded. On the contrary, the second thought to strike his hostess was that he looked unusually well. "Perhaps they've made it up?" thought Mrs. Prelude. But the hope died as soon as formed: Corinna would have been there. Friendship apart, there was nothing Corinna liked better than jumping on and off planes; also what husband with a wife available wouldn't on such a visit have brought her with him, if necessary by force? Sadly, Mrs. Prelude had to conclude the breach unhealed. Her next mental question was whether he knew she knew. If he did know she knew, wouldn't he be expectant of sympathy in return? Mr. van Hoyt's immediate launching into his eulogy of Arthur, without any reference to Corinna to start that sympathy's flow, suggested that he didn't know she knew; on the other hand it might have been tact—his own trouble so comparatively minor. Of course Mrs. Prelude could never tire of hearing Arthur eulogized, but by the time Mr. van Hoyt at last paused (having spoken completely without notes), she found she knew just what she was going to say, to give him at any rate the chance to open his heart and be sympathized with himself.

"You put it all so beautifully!" sighed Mrs. Prelude; and added, "Corinna wrote."

There was a brief silence. Mr. van Hoyt's expression changed. The light of generous enthusiasm faded from his eye; his cheek, hot with eloquence, paled. Mrs. Prelude thought it was like seeing a cloud pass over the sun.

"You know?"

His voice was low, but well under control. Mrs. Prelude nodded.

"I couldn't believe it!"

"She's in Mexico this minute."

"Mexico?"

"I divorce faster, in Mexico," explained Mr. van Hoyt wryly. "It'll still be legal."

"But how she can!" burst forth Mrs. Prelude. "Her letter upset me for days! You know I love Corinna dearly—but how she *can!*"

"I guess I was always too old for her," said Mr. van Hoyt.

"Nonsense!" cried Mrs. Prelude, impulsively pressing his hand. "Why, at every single conference I always thought you except for Arthur looked the youngest there!"

"You did?"

"Indeed I did!" affirmed Mrs. Prelude. (She wasn't flattering: Mr. van Hoyt, nudging sixty, was still more dapper than many a banker half a decade his junior. The fact that he was also a millionaire Mrs. Prelude barely glanced at, reprobating her foolish friend.) "Of course I'm much older than Corinna—"

"More mature," corrected Mr. van Hoyt.

"—but I'm sure that's not the reason! And you took her everywhere—"

"I did hope," recalled Mr. van Hoyt, "foreign travel might compensate."

"I meant, to the parties as well," said Mrs. Prelude. "Why, whatever more could she want?"

"It seems an action-painter," said Mr. van Hoyt. "She met up with this one in Athens. I guess it's a more glamorous occupation."

"If you ask *me*," said Mrs. Prelude warmly, "there's absolutely nothing more glamorous in the whole world than international finance. Packing Arthur's bags for him, I used to feel absolutely *privileged*."

"He was a much-envied man," said Mr. van Hoyt. "Corinna now—"

He checked himself: she was still technically his wife, and marital loyalty, in the circumstances highly creditable, forbade his detailing the many occasions, usually late at night, when it was he who'd packed for Corinna. After being the life and soul of an official soirée Corinna had the habit of flopping into bed and sleeping like a child. Instead—

"I don't know your own opinion of action-painting," offered Mr. van Hoyt, "but myself I can't seem to get the point."

"Nor could Arthur," sufficiently answered Mrs. Prelude.

"He said it was just a passing fad. —Oh, dear, will he be able to *support* her?"

"She has her own money," said Mr. van Hoyt.

"Of course that makes a difference," reflected Mrs. Prelude. "*I* hadn't a penny . . ."

"You hadn't?" asked Mr. van Hoyt wistfully.

"I owe Arthur everything in the world. I think that's how it ought to be, between a woman and her husband."

Again silence briefly fell as Mr. van Hoyt now pressed the hand of his hostess. The sympathy between them was almost tangible—cobweb-fine, but what is stronger than cobweb?

"Have you ever visited New England?" asked Mr. van Hoyt.

"No, only New York," said Mrs. Prelude. "We stayed at the Plaza. The room-service was wonderful."

"I've a small property there," said Mr. van Hoyt. "One day I'd like to show it you. —Darnation, there's my car come to take me back to the air-port."

At once—

"Have you your brief-case?" cried Mrs. Prelude. "Shall I cut you a few sandwiches? Arthur could never eat a thing they gave him, on the plane! Will your pyjamas be aired, when you get to the hotel? Are they the Jaeger kind? — But what silly questions," she checked, chided herself, "when you must have everything arranged!"

"They don't sound foolish to me," said Mr. van Hoyt, "and in fact I have never been asked a single one of them before."

The hired car (a Rolls) deferentially but with some

slight urgency hooted again. Mrs. Prelude and Mr. van Hoyt exchanged a last, or possibly interim, handclasp.

"May I have the privilege of calling again," asked Mr. van Hoyt, "before I leave Europe?"

"Please do!" begged Mrs. Prelude. "It's been so lovely, talking about Arthur!"

Only Corinna could have been disappointed by this termination of their re-encounter. ("Snap her up, sugar," had advised Corinna, "before some fat Swiss gets in first!") Mr. van Hoyt knew what he was about. He saw that Mrs. Prelude—treasure that she was, it was part of what made her such a treasure—needed time to readjust into the position of a woman remarriageable. It surprised him in fact to find her so perky already. In a couple of months more, he judged, she would happily fly back with him to Boston to help inaugurate a Chair of International Finance by himself endowed and named for his late colleague: thence to drive out and visit a small property including amongst other amenities a swimming-pool and several miles of woodland walks. He'd even picked a chaperone for the trip—one of the loveliest ladies on the Harvard faculty, upon whose tact he could also rely to let him lead Mrs. Prelude about those woodland walks alone. Not that the spot where he intended to propose was far from the house, he didn't want her to be tired; it just gave the best view of it.

5.

Like Joan of Arc Lydia knelt hearing voices in the bells; with only a slight effort of the imagination knelt not in jeans but in a peasant's heavy skirt; actually stumbled, as she at last rose, in its imaginary folds; and left the church so elevated and bemused, it took Toby several moments to convey to her the fact that her bicycle had been stolen.

7

WHERE TWO BICYCLES had been left against the gate, now there was only one. There stood Toby's decrepit machine inviolate; Lydia's brand-new chromium job had vanished.

"I suppose we'd better go to the police," said Toby uneasily.

Lydia blinked. She was still only just awaking to reality.

"My rucksack as well . . . But won't it hold us up for hours?"

"More like days," said Toby.

"And we can't spare days . . ."

"Better write it off and push on," decided Toby. "You can always hire another and buy gear at Chambérieu. At least we've plenty of cash."

No Briton abroad likes tangling with the police because they are not Bobbies. Lydia had some bemused idea of a complaint laid in form catching up with them after they got home and coming to the notice of William. Essentially, however, both cousins were motivated by the common generous impulse to push on without losing time before the one's father, the other's uncle, died of starvation in a shed.

2.

Toby had literally to push. Obviously he couldn't accommodate Lydia on his cross-bar; faithful as his steed might be, the double burden would simply have sent it to the knacker's. But at least, as he began to sweat, he could pile his jacket on top of his rucksack, and they made not bad progress.

"Has the station at Villeneuve a proper restaurant?" asked Lydia presently.

"If not, there'll be an *auberge* in the village," said Toby, "and we've bags of time."

"I shall have an *escalope*. What shall you have?"

"*Bifteck*," said Toby unhesitatingly. "Preceded by *hors d'oeuvres* and topped off by whatever's going—I hope, cherry tarts."

"Or wild strawberries," meditated Lydia.

Nothing so alleviates a foot-slog as discussing what one is going to eat at the end of it. Toby wheeling his bicycle, Lydia padding alongside, each challenging the other to think of extras (such as mushrooms on toast, *coeur à la crème*, and local cheeses), they had cheerfully completed the full necessary mile before they realized that they were lost.

It seemed impossible, even in the swift-falling dusk, on a *route nationale*. The only explanation was that at some point they must have turned off again. In any case, where should have twinkled before them the red and green lights of signal-boxes gleamed lancet windows high up in what

was evidently the turret of a château a good bit further on.
—At any rate the length of a drive further on; the point at
which they halted in dismay was beside a tall iron gate ajar
between pillars with griffins on top.

"We'd better take a look at the map," said Toby.

Fortunately one thing efficient about his bicycle was the
lamp. It was an excellent lamp, adequate to read any map
by down to smallest place-names and roads unfit for auto-
mobiles. That it now proved useless was simply because
Toby's jacket which had the map in the pocket had fallen
off.

"I'm extremely sorry," apologized Toby. "It's entirely my
fault. I should have lashed it on."

"Considering besides the map it's got all our money in
it," said Lydia, rather clearly, "I really think you might."

It was extraordinary how quickly darkness had become
complete: the moon not yet risen.

"Actually what bothers *me* more," said Toby, "is our
passports."

"One does, doesn't one, feel slightly naked without
them?" agreed Lydia politely.

Somewhere in the distance, probably in the château
grounds, an owl hooted. The double note had nothing
cousinly about it: sounded more like an ill omen.

"I'd better cycle back," said Toby. "You wait here."

"One thing I absolutely refuse," wailed Lydia, "is to be
left all alone in the dark in the middle of France."

At which moment, whether fortunately or not, up cycled
a local gendarme on his suspicious nightly round.

3.

In other circumstances they might have been almost glad to see him. They might even have reported the theft of Lydia's bicycle. But as he flashed a torch into their faces and roughly demanded to see their papers of identity (both he and M. le Maire having had quite enough of hitch-hiking beatniks), the awareness that they hadn't any papers inhibited. Lydia indeed definitely quailed; Toby, without going so far as to feel naked, recognized himself in the unusual position of being at a disadvantage. So he took the high, Etonian hand.

"*Actuellement,*" said Toby, "*nous cherchons l'habitat d'un Duc, père d'un de mes amis qui nous a invités pour une concurrence d'élégance à bicyclette. La mienne (classe historique) vous voyez; celle de mademoiselle, d'une délicatesse et beauté extrême, arrivera par camion. Evidemment c'est un peu difficile pour vous, vu nos habillements pas très chic; mais indiquez-nous seulement, comme j'ai dit, l'habitat du bon vieux Duc, et tout sera regularisé.*"

Whether convinced or not—whether he'd taken in a half of Toby's brilliant improvisation—the gendarme at any rate grasped the last sentence, and it sufficed.

"*Mais vous voilà!*" exclaimed the gendarme, indicating the high griffin-guarded gate.

4.

Just as on the train to Chambérieu, there appeared to be no alternative. The gate wasn't even shut. Toby wheeling his bicycle, Lydia padding alongside, they entered a stately drive. The gendarme followed.

An owl hooted again. Otherwise all was silent, under tall trees, between stretches of parkland sensed rather than seen. A faint beginning of moonlight merely transformed fallen branches into man-traps.

"Don't look round," said Toby, "but is he still there?"

"How can I see, without looking round?" objected Lydia.

"My good girl, haven't you a powder-compact?"

"No," said Lydia. "It was in my rucksack."

"Then look."

Lydia glanced nervously over her shoulder.

"Yes."

"Then we must proceed," said Toby.

They proceeded—the gendarme keeping a nicely calculated distance of some four yards behind. A few heat drops began to fall.

"I wonder where we'll sleep," said Lydia.

"With luck, in a ditch," said Toby.

"At the police station I dare say they've quite nice cells."

"Don't you believe it," said Toby. "A friend of mine once spent two nights in a French cell."

"What for?"

"Demonstrating," said Toby vaguely. "Push on."

Suddenly, somewhere to the right, a dog bayed. It was a peculiarly powerful bay, suggesting a peculiarly large and powerful dog. All three, Lydia and Toby in front, the gendarme behind, momentarily halted.

"The Hound of the Baskervilles," said Toby. —"*Le Chien des Baskerville!*" he called back. "*Sherlock Holmes, le Maigret de son age! Tu n'as pas peur, mon brave?*"

The gendarme approached closer, either for company or to keep a nearer eye on them. He also now seemed to be trying to communicate something urgent, but his patois was too thick for them to understand. It still conveyed, however, such a final threat, or warning, that moved by a common impulse Toby let his bicycle fall, Lydia clutched his hand, and together they raced for whatever sanctuary the château offered.

5.

Fortunately there was no difficulty in gaining admission. Even as they panted towards a great historic porch (heels thudding on the gravel, the Hound of the Baskervilles baying behind), light through an opening door streamed to meet them; some sort of manservant accepted their dishevelment unsurprised, and wordlessly led the way across a great historic hall to the historic saloon beyond.

To Toby and Lydia (fresh from the dark, blinking under too many chandeliers), it seemed crowded. In fact no more than half-a-dozen merrymakers delightedly converged upon them—the males in white tuxedos, the three females exquisitely if somewhat fantastically attired in gold-bordered sari, pyjamas of thin Liberty silk, and shift sewn with pearl paillettes. Above the sari rose the head of a pig, above paillettes and Liberty silk the heads of sheep and goat; above the white tuxedos those of boar, wolf and ram—Mrs. Armadale, who had rented the château for the summer, having decided to give a special fun-party for her intimates with the aid of a box of most ingenious rubber masks specially imported from New York.

8

"C OME IN, COME IN!" cried Mrs. Armadale—thrusting up her rubber snout to reveal features scarcely less plump and by no means less avid. "How sweet, how *young! —*Did we frighten you?"

"Yes," said Lydia, "very much. You looked so natural."

"I was terrified too," said Toby, but more politely, also taking a rapid survey of the three men now equally unmasked. Not one looked as though he could be *le bon vieux Duc*: their ages apparently between thirty and forty, and any degeneracy of feature due less to aristocratic in-breeding than to alcohol. Toby in fact appreciated the whole set-up (beginning with the off-hand manservant) pretty accurately; if he hadn't the grandson of a peer of France for friend he had the nephew of a marquis, and knew châteaux frequently rented to fun-loving foreigners in the season when moats began to smell like drains. So although this particular fun-party struck him as a bit hairy-hocked, because outside it was dark, and they had no money, and Lydia was very white—

"I'm afraid we've rather boobed," continued Toby apologetically. "We hoped the Duke (actually a friend of mine's grandfather) would put us up overnight. But of course we'll just move on."

"Don't think of it!" cried Mrs. Armadale warmly (and just as Toby had anticipated). "What's of course is that you'll stay as long as you like! —I'm Lalage, and these are Babs and Cécile and Bobo and Peter and Blimps. What are *your* names, you babes in the wood?"

"Susan and Harold," said Toby, "Blackwood. We're cousins—on a tour of France to improve our accents."

Mrs. Armadale's fat white countenance—it was really difficult to tell whether she was wearing a mask or not—creased to the eye-pockets in a delighted, conspiratorial smile. Even a few dimples appeared here and there, like pocks in lard.

"Which I for one don't believe a single moment!" she declared. "I believe you're eloping!"

Instantly the whole fun-party (which was indeed in danger of falling flat on its face, as after several hours of mixed drinking fun-parties often do) took up the idea with enthusiasm—sheep and goat, boar, wolf and ram crowding round, breathing gin into Toby's and Lydia's faces, sucking at their youth as at an elixir vitae or whiff of cocaine. "So obviously, so *terriblement* in love!" yearned Babs—then remembering her rôle as the party's ingénue wriggled with glee inside her pearl paillettes and unmasked to thrust a cheek thrice-lifted against Toby's mouth. —Cécile however was before her with an arm around his neck and small silvered goat-horns delicately nuzzling. Which of the men nuzzled Lydia she couldn't distinguish; only as boar, wolf and ram were they separately identifiable. Actually it was Bobo, even drunker than Peter or Blimps.

[77]

"I tell you what," giggled Bobo, "let's have a wedding! Darling Lalage, wouldn't it be rather *fun?*"

"It certainly would," beamed Mrs. Armadale, tears of pleasure in her eyes to see her guests all enjoying themselves once more. (With new toys; a new game.) "Only what about a minister? They both look to *me* like Episcopalians."

"Then just a bedding—*à la dix-huitième siècle!*" giggled Blimps. "Let's bed them in the bridal suite! Bags I cut the bride's staylace!"

"She isn't wearing any, you oaf!" giggled Bobo, running a mottled hand over Lydia's breasts and ribs and stomach. "Bags I strip her jeans!"

Across a couple of diamond bracelets—

"I haven't heard anyone say 'Bags I' since I left prep," observed Toby. "Or can one still get *Chums?*"

As much to his surprise as to Lydia's relief, Babs instantly, with an outraged cry of "I *knew* you'd never been to a public school!" slapped Bobo twice over the face— once open-palmed, once back-handed. The diversion however was only momentary: producing, as Bobo recoiled, a slight lull in which Mrs. Armadale could be heard murmuring "*Dix-huitième,* my favourite *siècle!*" —It was the cue for Peter and Blimps: well aware that no fun-party at which they figured must fall flat if they were ever to figure at one again, uttering the most *dix-huitième* cries they could think of—such as "*Holà!*" "*Vive le roi!*" and "*Le roi boit!*" —they were manhandling Lydia up a broad stair before Toby got Cécile's tongue out of his mouth.

"It really *is* the king's bedroom!" gasped Mrs. Armadale joyfully. "Now it's the Duke's, but some king or other really did sleep there once—the letting-agent in Paris swore it on my Gold Card. What luck for you darling babes you came *here!*"

Outside, across the width of the hall, Toby heard a chain rattle, bolts jar. The off-hand, disabused manservant evidently judged the fun-party complete. Toby took the stairs two at a time, scrummed past Peter and Blimps, pulled Lydia in through a door and thankfully discovered a bolt to that too.

9

I̲T WAS A DOOR remarkable enough to be exhibited, off its hinges, in any exposition of French domestic art. Great slabs of oak had been carved—possibly by the same hand that carved *le beau jubé?*—into classic linenfold panels separating and bordering which bands of vineleaves sprouted vernacular grotesques: a tendril that ended as a snake, instead of a grape-cluster the torso of a satyr. It was a door Ruskin could have devoted a whole chapter to. But what Toby and Lydia chiefly appreciated was its strength. Under the poundings of boar, wolf and ram it didn't so much as budge.

"Open up, let us in!" shouted Bobo. "We've got to put the bride to bed!"

"To put the groom into his night-shirt!" shrilled Babs.

"To see they both know the first position!" giggled Blimps. "Now, all together, boys and girls—"

"Let us in, let us in, let us in!" chanted the fun-party.

Fists battered rhythmically. Still the door didn't budge. Toby, who had been leaning against it, on the discovery of a second bolt to shoot drew away, and drew Lydia with him as far as he could: towards a window on the chamber's further side. —It was so deeply embrasured, it was like a

small separate room, or hidey-hole. Toby thrust Lydia
down on the seat and let her hold his hand.

"They really *are* beasts," panted Lydia.

"You were quicker than I," admitted Toby.

"Pulling me upstairs, those men didn't just pull me, they
sort of *fondled* me . . ."

"Probably as much as they're capable of," said Toby.
"The whole thing stinks of voyeurism. —I was wrestling
with Cécile," he apologized. "Cry on me if you like."

"They'd see through the keyhole," said Lydia bitterly.

"Only there isn't one," pointed out Toby. "Which must
be a bit of a sell."

Indeed beyond the door high words were being exchanged on the very point. "If they won't let us in at least
we could have *watched*," complained Babs. "Why you had
to pick a room without a keyhole—!" "Isn't it always the
bridal suite?" retorted Peter. —Which was true: the com-
munal fun-party instinct to desecrate aimed not only at
young love, but also at the dignity of aristocratic age; a
week earlier, the old Duke's chamber had seen the local
tart bedded with the local ponce. "You should still have
reflected!" accused Cécile. "Not to disappoint poor Lalage!"

Actually Mrs. Armadale had collapsed before reaching
the stairs at all; the charivari had to proceed without her.
Muffled first by the door, then by the breadth of the room,
to Lydia and Toby its graceless racket now scarcely penetrated. They had time to draw breath; to look about them,
at the great bed, curtained above a head-board carved with
a coat-of-arms, at the shining wardrobes and tallboys and
straight-backed chairs. They had time to look out of the

[81]

window, across a formal garden and stretch of lawn towards wilder parkland beyond. The moon was now up, and almost full; a leaden statue, probably of Flora, on the garden-boundary gleamed like silver; grass had the pile of grey velvet. Owl ceasing to hoot, dog to bay, all was silent; the air so still, each tree in the park reared serene from its blot of shadow without a twig stirring.

"Look," said Lydia. "There's a hare."

The window stuck a little, but Toby got it open. "Where?"

"On the other side of the lawn, sitting up."

"It's a rabbit."

"It's a hare, I can tell by his ears."

"I've kept hares," countered Toby.

"You shouldn't have been allowed, and anyway *I've* kept rabbits. Wait till he moves."

For a minute the whole moon-washed demesne waited with them. Then in a series of jack-knife leaps the long-eared shape bounded across an invisible ha-ha, again paused, reared almost erect, and vanished.

"It was a hare all right," admitted Toby. "Actually I didn't keep 'em for long."

"What did you do with them?" probed Lydia, rather censoriously.

"Let 'em loose in the Lake District. I remember their names were Hengist and Horsa."

" 'Strong-haunched Hengist.' —Look, there he goes again."

Both leaned out as far as they could. The stilly air scarcely baffed against their faces; all that broke the moon-drenched silence was their own light breathing. On a sigh,

Lydia turned back towards the room; only her sigh broke the silence within . . .

Somewhere below a clock struck twelve with the peculiar impressiveness of a clock that has the house to itself.

"Have they all *gone?*" whispered Lydia.

"Where to?" murmured Toby.

"Off to another fun-party . . . ?"

"We'd have heard cars."

"But it's all so quiet!"

"Perhaps they've just passed out . . ."

Both listened intently. In every dwelling-place night echoes the activity of day in creak of floor-board, gurgle of water-pipe, rattle of latch: the château was no more perfectly still than is an orchard on an apparently windless afternoon. (The chimes of the clock falling like over-ripe apples, its ticks the tiny tap of twig against twig.) The longer Toby and Lydia listened the more sounds they distinguished—but none of human origin.

"Bolt the door behind me," ordered Toby, "and don't open till I hoot."

2.

He was gone perhaps ten minutes. Lydia in the meantime inquisitively opened a few drawers. Their contents summed the chamber's double function as master-bedroom and bridal suite for fun-lovers: among ample flannel night-shirts crested like blazers, various small rubber devices which if Lydia was too innocent ever to have employed, she still wasn't too innocent to guess the use of . . .

"Monsieur le Duc, I tender my apologies," said Lydia aloud. —The phrase so pleased her histrionic ear, she repeated it several times in various attitudes, including a court curtsey. "La!" she added (dropping further back into the *dix-huitième*). "Should your grace e'er condescend to my own parents' humble home, I swear their purity of manners would quite delight you!" —Actually M. le Duc, in the current century, would have given his ears for Arthur Prelude's advice on investments whether the latter used contraceptives or not, and Lydia in her own character suspected so, but again it made a good line. Then she burst into tears. That she spoke of her father as though still alive reminded her that she believed him still alive—but shivering in what outhouse, toiling in what stony field? " 'Tis I, Lydia, your child!" cried Lydia—hastily exchanging hooped silk for the woollen but gem-embroidered mantle of Cordelia. But the part she'd always really wanted to play was Joan of Arc, and a moment later, in armour, straddled her recumbent parent (or Dunois) as with flashing sword she fended off an embattled Alpine small-holder (or King Hal). On the other side of the door Toby not only hooted, he had to bang. Lydia let him in with tears (Cordelia's) still wet on her cheeks, but also with Joan's hardy glance . . .

What immediately struck her was the fistful of notes he carried: both French and English.

"I was right," reported Toby, "they're absolutely strewn. It was like kicking one's way through dead bracken."

Lydia let the picturesque image pass.

"Where did you get that money?" she demanded. (Like all Preludes she took money seriously: whence obtained, what collateral, what interest.) "You don't mean to tell me you went through their pockets?"

"Only the chaps'," reassured Toby. "And I must say I was surprised: Bobo specialized in fivers. English and French together he must have had more than a hundred quid on him. The others I cleaned out just to play fair and get change for tips."

"Beasts as they are—" began Lydia.

"Of course I left I.O.U.s," said Toby virtuously. "Peter had a diary with a pencil. Now pull yourself together and let's push on."

3.

Half scandalized, half admiring, Lydia tiptoed after him down the great stair. It was indeed strewn, by the persons of Bobo, Peter and Blimps: what had given Toby the notion of dead bracken Lydia perceived to be the fading yellowish tan of their lolling faces and slack-wristed hands. —She trod with unnecessary precaution; only a hose-pipe would have aroused either them or the women strewn below—Cécile and Babs entwined on one settee, Mrs. Armadale, her enormous rump reared pathetic and disgraceful as a stranded sea-lion's, on her face beside the other breathing stertorously.

"I don't know about you," said Toby, "but personally I need a gargle. Come on!"

To his surprise, his cousin hesitated.

"The pig-face one was rather kind. At least she started out by meaning to be. And I'm sure she's a put-on pig . . ."

"Obviously they're all living on her," agreed Toby, "even miserly old Bobo." (This was in a sense unjust; Bobo no more than Blimps or Peter possessed a bean, he had simply been systematically picking Mrs. Armadale's purse, and desk, over the last couple of months.) "Anyway it's her own funeral," added Toby, "if she likes to pay for it."

Still Lydia paused.

"If Babs and Cécile wake first, they'll laugh at her . . ."

"My good girl, they've probably been laughing at her for years. Come on!"

"By the way she's breathing she'll probably have a stroke or something . . ."

"Oh, all right," said Toby. "But bags I," he quoted ironically, "cut her staylace."

Together, and they could have done with a third, they heaved Mrs. Armadale up and onto the couch. Beneath the sari her fabulously expensive foundation-garment turned out to be controlled not by laces but by zip: as often in an emergency, it stuck. Toby's penknife however operated so successfully (slitting down about eighteen inches of fabulously expensive, specially woven nylon), the resultant bursting-forth of grateful flesh at once startled and reassured. Unconsciously groaning with relief Mrs. Armadale felt her stomach spread to its natural circumference; and with no more than natural snores sank yet deeper into drunken slumber.

"She's such a fool," said Lydia compassionately.

"I still need a gargle," said Toby. "Now for heaven's sake come *on*—unless," he added, again with irony, "you want to kiss her?"

Lydia did so. One of the qualities that were in time to

make her a very great actress indeed—to make her Mistress
Quickly a minor classic—in fact germinated at that moment, as in fat, drunken Mrs. Armadale she recognized,
and saluted, a smatch of earth's grubby casual benevolence;
and gave her a kiss before helping Toby unbar the door.

4.

Another example of earth's benevolence: Toby, finding his
bicycle where he had dropped it, wheeled it no more than a
yard or two before both pedals fell off (he had dropped it
rather hurriedly), and after collecting his rucksack abandoned the machine on the grass beside the drive. The
château gardener, immediately too cautious to snaffle it, as
it rusted found it awkward to mow round; through its
spokes sprang up a fine crop of nettles. Nettles attract
nightingales; for years after M. le Duc was able to lead his
own guests, after dinner, to enjoy *le chant du rossignol*. On
one particularly delightful occasion a famous cellist both
allured and accompanied: Lydia's apologies were made for
her by a nightingale.

5.

In a ditch indeed slept Toby and Lydia; but the night was
warm and the ditch dry. Their youth, and fatigue, were
better than barbiturates; both slept like logs, and under the
early sun woke fresh as daisies. The sensible decision to
retrace their steps to the station where they originally got

off, not only because they knew they could catch a train there, but also on the chance of finding Toby's jacket, involved some four miles on empty stomachs, but neither flinched. —By daylight they saw easily how they'd lost their way: the elbow from the *route nationale* towards the château gate was almost as broad, if less well maintained between ditch and hedgerow, as the highway itself.

"I've been thinking," said Toby. "I'm pretty sure it happened after we turned off."

"After it got dark," said Lydia, with a shiver.

"Exactly. Before, we'd have noticed. Unless the locals hereabouts get up damn' early, it's evens we'll find it."

"Then we'll have to go back and redeem those I.O.U.s," said Lydia (a Prelude still even in torn jeans and with grass-seed in her hair). But she shivered again; thought she saw Toby shiver. Hitherto, by common unspoken consent, and as children suppress the memory of a nightmare, neither had referred to the events of the previous night-time hours. —Her sharp eye caught by a patch of orange protruding from a rabbit-hole, Lydia almost looked away again . . .

Their courage however was not to be tested. It was Toby's jacket, all right; but though their passports were still in the pocket, their money wasn't.

"I must say whoever got up early was pretty decent," said Lydia gratefully.

"A simple peasant," observed Toby, "probably hasn't any use for passports."

"No, but he might have for a jacket," said Lydia.

If it crossed Toby's mind that an expensive orange skiing jacket on the back of a simple peasant would be a highly

questionable object, he didn't say so. He felt Lydia's innocence something to be preserved as long as possible.

Again they didn't go to the police. As Toby pointed out,
they had absolutely no proof that the money was ever
there. (No I.O.U.s, for example.) In any case, they weren't
short: at an inn outside the station, if too early for *biftecks*
and *escalopes*, the cousins consumed an enormous breakfast of omelettes, rolls, more omelettes, more rolls, butter
and honey and coffee. Toby tipped the waiter so lavishly, as
they boarded the train the man pressed on them a bag of
slightly over-ripe plums and returning to his wife in the
kitchen rejoiced that there were still a few milords left
alive.

"*Fagottés comme ça?*" sniffed his wife.

"*C'est le genre beatnik,*" explained the waiter.

10

IN LONDON, ALICE was letting William buy her an engagement-ring. Hitherto she'd always refused one, she said she hated wearing rings, but William, with twenty thousand pounds behind him, was masterful. He still wasn't prepared to sink a quarter of his capital in a square-cut emerald, and felt annoyed with the assistant at Cartier's who encouraged Alice to try one on.

"Isn't it the most beautiful thing you've ever *seen?*" breathed Alice.

"Not to be crude," observed the assistant carelessly, "also a remarkably sound investment . . ."

"I'm not looking for a sound investment," said William.

No more, to do her justice, was Alice. The jujube of green fire, as she'd said, was simply the most beautiful thing she ever saw, and Alice loved beauty. It was one of the reasons why she loved the Ritz: peace and quiet apart, the dining-room at the Ritz—spacious under gilded swags, looking out upon a park—is possibly the most beautiful in Europe. Towards the beauty of wildflowers and sunsets and so on Alice felt less strongly; she rarely paused long before a buttercup. Her passion was still a true one—just rather specialized.

The square-cut emerald laid aside, she didn't seem to care to look at anything else. William was glad. Only the besotment of love could have induced him into Cartier's at all: he had in fact already arranged for a delightful little antique job, a sapphire surrounded by rose-diamonds, to be awaiting Alice's inspection at a lesser jeweller's further on. Alice in turn now docilely followed William, and made him happy by approving his choice at once. Over lunch under the gilded swags she allowed him to place it, with some slight tender ceremony, on her finger, and exclaimed how perfectly it fitted. "The ladies of the *Ancien Régime*," said William, tenderly, and forgetting how Alice was accustomed to hurtle her jeep about, "had useless little hands too . . ." "Please, can I have been a Marquise?" smiled back Alice . . .

She was still rather quiet; pensive. The occasion was of course in a way solemn, and William was glad, again, that she evidently felt it so. The ensuing silence disturbed him only on account of the waiter. Many who lunch or dine at the Ritz feel a need to sparkle, at least while being served. It takes the regulars—the Greek ship-owners, the American art-dealers—to sit unperturbed in total silence. (Mr. Xerxes and Madame rarely exchanged a word—the one absorbed in the *Financial Times*, the other in a Book of the Month.) William was as yet so to speak uninitiated; and seeking some topic of conversation pitched on a telephone-call from his mother received that morning.

"D'you know what?" said William. "You may well be going to have a millionaire step-papa-in-law."

Alice looked interested at once. The waiter was naturally

too well trained to, but William sensed a heightened respect. It had been his aim in throwing in "millionaire"— a word sparkling in itself.

"Tell me more, darling," said Alice.

"It seems that Mr. van Hoyt, a colleague of my late father's, flew in for an hour's chat between Zürich and Amsterdam."

Alice opened wide brown eyes.

"Zürich and Amsterdam?"

"Precisely. Mother described it as a visit of condolence; but of course they chatted about this and that as well, such as the van Hoyt divorce. He's to call again before he leaves Europe. —I honestly don't believe Mother has a clue," added William, "but one can't help suspecting intentions on the part of Father's pal . . ."

"Then I think it's perfectly dreamy," said Alice, "when your mother's such a sweetie-pie." She paused. "Really and truly cross-your-heart a millionaire?"

"Multi," said William—the waiter again at his elbow. "I dare say he owns half Bermuda."

"Bermuda must be beautiful," sighed Alice. "All those luxury hotels with their own swimming-pools . . ."

For a moment William actively disliked her. She slipped her hand into his; he still disliked her. She pressed her nails into his palm, and he felt weak with love. As his sister Elizabeth had observed, he was fixated. He was a one-woman man. His mother had his affection, he was quite fond of young Lydia, otherwise he was all Alice's. —Why he suddenly thought of Lydia, at that moment, was probably due to the fact that when she'd kept rabbits, and tried to make him fondle them, just so had their hard little claws dug. Absently, William hoped she was enjoying herself.

2.

"How much longer?" muttered Lydia, attempting to discourage an urchin from her lap without giving offense to its mother, father, grandmother or aunt.

"Only half-an-hour," encouraged Toby.

The holiday-time train was so full they hadn't been able to sit next to each other, only opposite, squeezed amongst two French families, their hand-luggage and food parcels. It was very hot, in the narrow third-class compartment. All windows were shut. The two fathers chain-smoked caporal. Once an hour by their watches Toby and Lydia made a sortie into the corridor; but they'd made some five already, and each displacement aroused increasing animosity. The moment they stood up, infants, hand-luggage and food parcels overflowed into their vacant seats; on their return they were glared at as though they'd never been seen before. They would have stayed in the corridor, but that the corridor was full too and Lydia got her behind pinched. As for the refreshment car, they couldn't approach it. Lydia saw easily why her neighbours had brought food parcels, but the chumping of garlic-flavoured sausage combined with the smell of caporal was making her feel sick.

The urchin clambering up her knee actually was sick.

—Only just in time Lydia shoved it off to be sick on the floor.

"*On voit bien que mademoiselle n'aime pas les petits!*" rebuked the mother.

"*Les Anglais ont toujours le coeur dur, pour leurs enfants!*" snapped the aunt.

It was an interesting illustration of Elizabeth's remark to William on the day of the funeral: ever since the Tudors, hadn't the English treatment of their young moved to scandalized pity, scandalized indignation, across-Channel contemporaries? Elizabeth upon such a modern instance might have based a quite printable paper about the persistence of national images. Lydia, her mind less well stored, and certainly less well balanced, could only shut her eyes and count the minutes until the train halted at Chambérieu.

3.

Certain common traits run in all families, if skippingly. The mind of Toby, for his age, was almost as well balanced as Elizabeth's. During the long hot train journey (absolutely no moonshine), he had been thinking steadily and practically; and had waited to inform Lydia of his conclusions only because he didn't want a row with her in the compartment. As soon as they left the station, however, he halted and took the bull by the horns.

"We now," stated Toby, "head straight for H. M. Consul."

As he expected, his cousin turned on him in an indignation not for long speechless.

"You must be mad," said Lydia. "You must be lunatic. And a rat. Didn't we agree right from the start to keep grown-ups out of it?" —The word "grown-ups" was a mistake, as she instantly recognized; it gave Toby the chance to smile almost as William or Elizabeth would have smiled. "What I mean," said Lydia, "is that I fail to see why you've suddenly gone all Foreign Office."

"Because in the first place," said Toby stubbornly, "he obviously knows the country better than we do. He might save us days trekking up to well-known beauty-spots. He may even have heard something, some chat after the crash there seemed no point in investigating with the air-line all hunky-dory."

"Then he's another rat."

"In addition," said Toby, "I think he should be given a chance to aid and comfort before we make him look a pretty complete fool. After all, it's his career."

"Brother-rats," nodded Lydia.

"What doesn't seem to strike you," said Toby patiently, "is that it's never even been suggested to him that Uncle Arthur isn't dead. Of course if we can't get him to believe us—which I admit may be pretty difficult—we're back to square one. On my own I wouldn't try it; I dare say he wouldn't believe you either . . ."

So was Lydia won over. The prospect of not exactly kneeling at the Consul's feet (as Isabella at the feet of Duke Vincentio: *Measure for Measure*), but of at least smiting him with her eloquence like Portia in *The Merchant of Venice* (and thus proving Toby wrong besides), was irresistible. Only at Toby's next suggestion, that she'd better buy herself a skirt because they didn't want to look like a couple of beatniks, did she show her teeth again.

"Just for that," snarled Lydia, "I shall ruin us at a *boutique* . . ."

11

SHE DIDN'T, HOWEVER. Apart from the fact that Chambérieu afforded no *boutiques*, as soon as their debate was settled all the familiar sense of urgency descended again. After so much time lost already Lydia bought her skirt, or rather a cotton frock, off a hanger at the first shop they came to and changed into it in the downstairs ladies' room of Le Grand Hôtel de Chambérieu et de l'Europe while Toby deposited his rucksack. She would have liked a bath (*chambres avec bain*, offered Le Grand Hôtel), but it was getting on for five, and they didn't know what time the consulate closed.

"How do I look?" Lydia paused to ask nevertheless.

Toby regarded her seriously. He belonged to the new, surprising generation of British males genuinely interested in style. His own rig of period knickerbockers and skiing jacket was as carefully calculated as a piece of op-art. Contemplating Lydia in a black-and-white check several sizes too large for her, but which she'd kilted up under the bosom with its scarlet belt—

"One thing I will say for you," complimented Toby, "you know how to wear clothes."

Lydia was always to know how to wear clothes. —Issued

[97]

an out-sized nightdress, as Wendy (her first West End rôle, in *Peter Pan*), Lydia kilted that up too, with a dressing-gown cord; and if a Tanagra figurine wasn't exactly what Sir James Barrie had envisaged, a producer who saw her subsequently offered her the part of Miranda in *The Tempest*.

2.

It wasn't much of a consulate to which the cousins were directed. It was in fact a rather down-at-heel villa with on the door-step two bottles of milk still waiting to be taken in, also a melting block of ice. In the lobby a plump young Frenchman nodded over a typewriter; the Consul's office beyond reassured distressed British nationals chiefly by back-numbers of *Punch* and *Country Life* piled on a chair opposite the consular desk. Nor was Mr. Dumbly (so the plump secretary mumbled his name) much of a consul. Great Britain is in general well served by her representatives, British-born or not: most know at least on which side their bread is buttered; certain heroes of the breed have stood embattled against riot and revolution even with the phone cut off. Mr. Dumbly (if such was his name) looked unlikely to be one of them. His most noticeable feature was his paunch. He wore no waistcoat—in the heat understandable, but it made his paunch all the more conspicuous as he swivelled in his chair to regard the cousins inimically.

"If it's your fares home, no," he said at once. "Hitch-hike here, hitch-hike back."

"Sir—" began Toby.

"And don't come your school-tie over me either," said

Mr. Dumbly. "Half of 'em bought at a haberdasher's in Brighton."

"I see you wear Winchester," agreed Toby suavely, removing the papers so that Lydia could sit down. "This is m' cousin Miss Prelude."

Mr. Dumbly (if such was his name) slightly straightened. He hadn't yet forgotten the hell of a to-do over a chap called Prelude after the plane crash—evidently some sort of a V.I.P. Mr. Dumbly disliked V.I.P.s on principle; in his opinion they had too much cheek. One V.I.P. (in the Foreign Office as it turned out, and Mr. Dumbly only wished he'd known sooner) had had the cheek to tick him off, and even threaten relegation, simply because he didn't always take the milk in. What Mr. Dumbly liked were decent quiet couples on a package-trip who just needed directing to the Anglican church. But though he mentally groaned, he sat up and regarded Lydia with wary respect.

"Miss Prelude? It was I who had the sad privilege," recalled Mr. Dumbly, "of escorting your dear mother on that last sad, er, tour of inspection. How is the poor lady?"

"Actually very well," said Lydia, "and actually why I and m' cousin are here is because we think she made a mistake."

3.

This time Mr. Dumbly groaned aloud. They weren't the first to come pestering him with foolish hopes. "If only relatives would trust the air-line!" thought Mr. Dumbly—quite unaware of any irony. "God knows *they* want to keep the death-roll down!" —He put on his waistcoat. Out of the breast-pocket fell two cigars, one intact, one nipped short for future use; both deriving from M. le Maire, who even more than Mr. Dumbly disliked the prospect of any further investigation and possible publicity. However unfairly, an air-crash does a holiday resort no good. It spoils the holiday-image.

"My dear Miss Prelude," said the Consul firmly, "take my word for it: there isn't a chance."

And Lydia hadn't a chance. The arguments with which she had convinced her cousin on Mr. Dumbly made no impression whatever. He let her repeat them simply because she was Miss Prelude; though he still sat more or less upright, he wasn't listening. (Even Portia wouldn't have had a chance.) The Consul simply closed his mind. It was a method he frequently employed when pestered: just close the jolly old mind. Any slight thought that now crossed it concerned whether to light the stub-cigar as soon as the young idiots left or reserve it, as he'd intended, until after dinner. As Lydia's voice began to tremble, as she grew more and more impassioned, he decided on the first course; he felt the jolly old nerves were going to need soothing . . .

"—So you see what it means to us!" finished Lydia passionately.

"I do indeed," said Mr. Dumbly, opening his eyes. (Or hadn't he shut them? He hoped not; he couldn't remember.) "I've never in all my born days been more touched and distressed. But so long as you didn't actually *know* you were smuggling—"

He checked himself. Lydia rose.

"I'm afraid there's only one word for it," said Mr. Dumbly hurriedly. "*Requiescat.*"

4.

In the now-empty lobby it was some moments before Toby could meet his cousin's eye.

"At least," observed Lydia, "you've—what is it?—played a straight bat. *Floreat Etona.*"

"I've a good mind to have him carpeted," said Toby angrily.

They went out past the milk-bottles and the ice and walked on in silence. Presently a corner brought them to the town's central promenade: gravelled between rows of elms, flanked on either side, across the road, by shops and *bistros*. Some of the latter had colonized under the trees with a scattering of iron chairs and small round tables, few as yet occupied; Toby and Lydia could sit where they chose. Their parent-*bistro*, so to speak, turned out to be one of the more modest establishments, Le Café des Abeilles, but its waiter ran out with flattering speed to take their order for a carafe of red wine. Each would secretly have preferred lemonade, or even tea, only they badly needed to assert their sophistication.

"What can one expect, outside Paris?" observed Lydia, in travelled tones.

"I believe there's quite a decent chap at Lyon," said Toby.

Lydia took a swig of wine and relapsed slightly.

"All the same, what a *beast!*"

[*101*]

"Oaf," corrected Toby.

"Very well, oaf-beast."

Toby hesitated.

"Oaf-beast or not, he seemed pretty positive . . ."

"At the end I don't believe he was even listening," said Lydia. "You mean he simply won't admit to having been involved in a ghastly mistake. He'd rather let poor Father starve. If you want to give up—"

"Not I," said Toby. "We'd better have something to eat."

The waiter at his signal rushed up with a broad menu, unhesitatingly took orders for *bifteck* and *escalope* and returned with hard-boiled eggs. —A plaque adorning the façade of Le Grand Hôtel, on the promenade's opposite side, welcomed voyagers to *le pays du Brillat-Savarin;* but it was simpler, if less sophisticated, to eat than to argue.

"Actually I rather like hard-boiled eggs," said Toby.

"Oh, so do I," said Lydia. "They put nothing on the waist-line."

Both drank some more red wine. Contrary to their expectations, it didn't particularly exhilarate. In the elms overhead a few strings of fairy-lights, subsidized by the municipality to promote tourism, experimentally flickered and went out. Lydia sighed.

"I'm sorry," apologized Toby. "It was my idea."

"*I* didn't give much of a performance," acknowledged Lydia. "I wasn't projecting myself properly. Anyway, I'd still much rather we were on our own . . ."

She yawned. So, to his surprise, did Toby. It wasn't quite eight o'clock, but they'd both had a long day. —That Lydia's black-and-white check was ample as her Wendy night-dress proved just as well, for she slept in it. Toby checked them both in at Le Grand Hôtel (*chambres avec bain*), where he'd deposited his rucksack. So slender an amount of baggage the receptionist rather raised an eyebrow at, until Toby drew on Blimps's pickings to pay in advance; after which, and after drawing off most of the hotel's hot water, the cousins slept for twelve solid hours and woke once more fresh as daisies to begin their search.

12

"I'VE HAD A LETTER from Mother," said Elizabeth, idly stretching her newly tanned legs upon a Grecian shore. As her lover appreciated, they were classic legs; i.e., slightly shorter from knee to hip than was currently modish, but also offering a broader, more accommodating cradle. Paying tribute with a slight scattering of gold-dust sand—

"And what does she say, in her letter?" asked Henry Alcott.

"That Mr. van Hoyt's been to call. —One of Father's millionaire colleagues," explained Elizabeth, idly. "He dropped in to tea between Zürich and Amsterdam."

"A very nice gesture."

"Mother's terribly distressed because his wife's left him," added Elizabeth. "She's getting a Mexican divorce to marry an action-painter she met in Athens."

"The background to international banking sounds more fascinating than one suspected," said Henry. "Do many such amours blossom?"

"They were on holiday," said Elizabeth defensively. —As though the brief-case her father carried, that all his colleagues carried, contained besides computerized statistics the commandment *Thou shalt not let thy wife run off the rails*. Then seeing Henry laughing at her, she laughed in turn. "Prig that I am," said Elizabeth. "Actually Mother seems to have sown a little seed of love herself—not consciously, of course; but one doesn't lightly fly in for tea between Zürich and Amsterdam. . . . You wouldn't actually mind, would you, having him in the family?"

This was in fact the first time she had ever hinted at any legalizing of their amour. Hitherto they'd been simply two free souls releasing a common atavistic urge on a short sybaritic holiday. (The phrase now a jest between them; the adjective sybaritic equally applicable to a moment of passion and an inferior kebab.) But in telling William she wanted no more from her lover, Elizabeth had lied. She wanted a wedding-ring. It happens to the freest of souls, especially if female; Elizabeth's distinction lay in the fact that it wasn't her own future she wished to secure, so much as Henry's.

William was only partly right in his judgment of his elder sister. Undeniably Elizabeth disliked taking second place; undeniably took pride in her own attainments; her bossiness was still basically a variant of her mother's instinct to cherish. Picking brilliant non-starters, Elizabeth genuinely wished to get them started. (With the Alistair remembered by William she almost succeeded. He was a scene-designer. When Covent Garden semi-commissioned sets for a new ballet, Elizabeth herself went on the waggon. It was the Scotland versus France rugby-match in Dublin that prevented the maquettes being completed to date.) By this time, however, after four or five years of such experimentings, Elizabeth believed she would have a better chance of success in lawful wedlock. A lover, weary of being cherished, all too easily slung his hook—slipped back, like Alistair, into the comfortable wash of failure, leaving nothing but wasted pains behind him—whereas a husband Elizabeth fancied one could really get down to work on. . . .

She still spoke lightly; and as lightly her lover answered.

"Aren't you my little rich girl already?" joked Henry Alcott.

Though the phrase was ambiguous, Elizabeth felt satisfied that he'd at least been given food for thought; as indeed he had, though in a direction that would have surprised her. —Siblings know a great deal about each other, but not all; as William misjudged Elizabeth, so did Lydia the pair of them. Neither was mercenary. However welcome their inheritances, neither for the sake of twenty thousand pounds would have left their father starving in a shed. Upon any solid ground for believing him still alive, they would have been as active in search after him as Lydia. There was no solid ground. Lydia, rightly judging her brother and sister relieved by the fact, was still wrong to accuse them of mercenariness. Elizabeth genuinely flinched from the ghoulishness of an exhumation order, William before the prospect of all those wreaths to be sent back with little notes. Of course they were relieved that there was no solid ground; but would have been just as much so, inheriting twopence apiece.

Nor did either easily suspect mercenariness in others; as William at the Ritz had introduced Mr. van Hoyt to impress not so much Alice as the waiter, so now Elizabeth introduced him simply as a peg on which to hang the hitherto unmentionable word family. But in each case the Preludes reckoned without their hearers. It was another trait they shared.

Elizabeth had in fact promoted her ambitions better than she knew. She might be her lover's little rich girl already, but twenty thousand pounds barely made an heiress even in Wycherley's day; moreover Henry Alcott couldn't but be aware of several glances directed towards his own long limbs by obviously better-heeled female tourists bickering with their gigolos. In shanghaiing her lover to Greece, Elizabeth had carelessly exposed him to moral dangers quite unknown in Fleet Street, and which if she didn't recognize, Henry did. He had indeed developed rather a contempt for the gigolos, letting themselves be fee'd with gold cigarette-cases and Charvet shirts, or at the limit a sports-car, when they might have aimed at a settlement. He wasn't, he told himself mercenary; it was simply that he wished to devote himself to literature, not journalism. When he thought of the great Proustian novel he might write, living as Proust lived, above financial care, to marry very much more money than Elizabeth's appeared almost a duty. At the same time the gigolo-toters (most of them strong-arming middle-age at least) aroused a certain wholesome distaste in him; it came as a beautiful thought that as other millionaires endowed hospitals or art-galleries, Mr. van Hoyt might care to endow, so to speak, a literary masterpiece—especially if written by one of the family. Rather echoing Alice, whom he'd never seen—

"An honest-to-God bloody millionaire?" meditated Henry Alcott.

"You might write a Profile of him," suggested Elizabeth —a little surprised, but as always helpful.

Well, perhaps, as a latch-lifter, thought Henry Alcott.

"If your mother's going to be consoled, three cheers," he said aloud. "I've always liked the sound of her. Shall I oil your back?"

Gold-dust scattered again as Elizabeth turned over. Her long black hair, half unpinned, fell in sleek arabesques far more beautiful, thought Henry gratefully, than any wig from Charles of the Ritz. . . .

"Has anyone ever told you you had classic shoulder-blades?" he asked fondly.

"Yes; a man at the Marylebone Public Baths," said Elizabeth. "He trained swimmers for the Olympics. But I do agree, darling, it's quite enormously pleasant that Mother, who really needs a husband, may have found someone she really likes so soon."

"Three cheers again," said Henry. "I only hope she likes her son-in-law."

Elizabeth so reassured him on the point, next day she was wearing an engagement-ring. If but of silver, it was still very engaging: an ancient coin set in a modern bezel minutely incised with dolphins: wearing which Elizabeth stretched more happily still on the fabled Grecian shore.

2.

Professor Harvill, calling on Mrs. Prelude, had refrained from inviting Alice to drive him over in her jeep. In the first place he thoroughly mistrusted the vehicle, and in the second, his object being more or less to put his hostess through a viva, he remembered how Alice could sabotage a tutorial. Prudently, solo, Professor Harvill entrained; and reached the house at Chesham Bois, if at the unconventional hour of two-thirty, intact and unencumbered.

He arrived also unheralded. It hadn't occurred to him that Mrs. Prelude might be from home; she was no gadabout. His opinion of her (in this as in all things) proved justified; she opened the door herself—in an apron, for she had actually just washed up lunch and was in the middle of preparing dinner.

Her welcome was nonetheless genuine. She had been thinking about him, and feeling for him, off and on ever since receiving his two letters; on sight, her sympathy increased. Mrs. Prelude would have felt for any widower faced by all the problems incident to a daughter's marriage, but somehow Professor Harvill's neat brown whiskers gave him an extra pathos, for she perceived at once that he'd been trying to dye them.

"How nice of you to come!" exclaimed Mrs. Prelude warmly. "I expect it's to talk about the wedding?"

For a moment Professor Harvill was thoroughly startled. If his own thoughts had surprised him by their forwardness, how far and fast must his hostess's have been travelling? ("And without the slightest encouragement!" thought Professor Harvill, almost censoriously.) A second moment however made all plain, as Mrs. Prelude added that of course she would be delighted to help with dear Alice's trousseau.

"Just to see she doesn't forget dull things like hankies," explained Mrs. Prelude. "I'm sure Alice has wonderful taste! —Would you terribly mind coming into the kitchen? I'm in the middle of a stew."

In some relief Professor Harvill followed. It still annoyed him that Alice, even absent, had so to speak managed to butt in already, and he decided to make his attitude towards her plain without delay.

"Don't for a minute," said Professor Harvill, even while accepting a glass of milk and a digestive biscuit (all Mrs. Prelude could think of to offer him at that awkward hour), "imagine that I'd have had her exposed on a hillside. It never entered my mind."

"Alice? Good gracious, of course not!" exclaimed Mrs. Prelude. "Of course babies, when they cry, can be upsetting to any man who has to think at home—when Arthur was thinking I used to rock Elizabeth, and then William, half the night—"

"But could you keep them out of his study?" interposed Professor Harvill—his mind leaping from the young Preludes' infancy to their adolescence.

"I kept *everyone* out of Arthur's study. Then, it was really just the spare bedroom," recalled Mrs. Prelude fondly, "but I still made it *sacred*—and of course we never had anyone to stay. Dear Alice I can well believe was sometimes tiresome, but I'm sure you're devoted to her."

Alice's father, who had been about to explain, following the defence that he wouldn't have exposed her on a hillside, that his feelings towards her were now so more than cool, her trousseau was a matter of perfect indifference to him, decided to let the whole thing slide. He didn't want to lose Mrs. Prelude's good opinion, however mistakenly (in both senses of the term) based. Moreover his attention was just then distracted.

"Dear Alice!" repeated Mrs. Prelude. "And my lucky William! —You won't mind if I just brown the onions?"

The odour as she popped a knob of butter into a hot frying-pan and then tipped in a plateful of onion-rings was the most delicious Professor Harvill had ever smelled. His late wife had been as indifferent to cookery as Alice was; only at High Table, for years, had he enjoyed a meal worth saliva. Nose alerting palate, he almost licked his chops.

"I brown the carrots too," explained Mrs. Prelude, observing with pleasure his interested look, "and just a little parsnip. The steak and kidney's on already, but I put in the bay-leaves later . . ."

With what grace she lifted the lid of a large iron casserole already a-simmer above a bead of gas!

"Then how long d'you cook it?" asked Professor Harvill.

"Four hours," said Mrs. Prelude. "It's stewing-steak."

"Then you make apple-pies, and so on?"

"Well, not this afternoon," smiled Mrs. Prelude. "Barbara—Miss Hume, who's staying with me—wants me to type out some poodle-pedigrees for her."

She could type as well.

"Latin," hazarded Professor Harvill (his own lecture-notes as often as not illegible), "shouldn't by comparison present much difficulty?"

"Not if written out clearly first," said Mrs. Prelude, "as Arthur always did. I must have typed *quantilla prudentia* over and over again."

"A common tag," said Professor Harvill, rather jealously,

"if not unuseful. *Quantilla prudentia orbs regnatur!* —We are governed by fools."

"I always thought it had something to do with insurance companies," confessed Mrs. Prelude. "How nice it is to know!"

All men, even if not professors, enjoy instructing. Professor Harvill warmed to her more and more.

"With a simple grammar, and a little coaching, you'd soon get the hang," he promised kindly. "As an occupation for quiet evenings I can think of none more pleasant."

"Neither can I," agreed Mrs. Prelude. "Of course dear Alice will be in white? Do tell her that of course I'll come out of mourning for the wedding-day!"

Any man whatever might have been excused for not recognizing her in mourning as it was. Mourning has never applied to aprons, and Mrs. Prelude's, protecting her thin black for Rome, was practically rowdy with pink roses. Professor Harvill scarcely took in her meaning; only realized with fresh annoyance that Alice had butted in again. —He scowled; Mrs. Prelude, remembering how Arthur had always hated to be bothered about clothes, decided to wait for Alice herself, who was in any case due to be staying with those friends in the neighbourhood during the following week . . .

Instinct, or again the memory of Arthur, warned her equally from the topic of the reception. "Then what did he come for?" Mrs. Prelude asked herself. "If not to talk about the wedding?" She was surprised, but by no means put out. It was nice to have someone in the kitchen with her, especially a man. Mrs. Prelude didn't precisely formulate the second half of this thought, but she in fact kept

Professor Harvill in the kitchen for an early cup of tea and tossed him off a few hot scones while letting him instruct her in a simple Latin declension. —Beginners are customarily started on "*Amo*, I love"; with for him unusual sensitivity, Professor Harvill substituted *Habeo*. He had already awarded Mrs. Prelude an alpha plus.

3.

"You've made eleven mistakes, dear," chided Barbara gently. "The same nearly every time: Apricot Mignonettes are of *Hartfield*, not Harvard."

"I'm so sorry," apologized Mrs. Prelude. "I must have had my mind on the stew."

"Which is simply delicious," said Miss Champney. "Why on earth can't you learn to type yourself?"

It was the regrettable fact that in this spell of comparative idleness and luxury the friends had begun to bicker a little; all at once, Mrs. Prelude thought perhaps Arthur wouldn't want her to keep them much longer. . . .

For some reason, about this time, she was dreaming of Arthur with unusual vividness. They were rather disturbing dreams, always following the same pattern: she had done something Arthur disapproved of, only he wouldn't say what. She had to guess. It was like a nightmare-dream of Twenty Questions—only worse, because unless she guessed right at the first the train (sometimes it was an aeroplane), would leave without her. —Was it Arthur's inhaling-apparatus she'd mislaid? Her own umbrella? Had he returned to the hotel to find her absent? However narrowly, in dreams, Mrs. Prelude examined her conscience, it was clear on every point—which only made matters worse. It came as a sudden and beautiful thought that dear Arthur wasn't bothering about the past at all, but the present . . .

"I've had them quite long enough," reflected Mrs. Prelude of her unsuspecting friends; and determined to drop a couple of dismissive hints, such as "How quickly elections come round," or "What a pity to lose your clientèle," at the first opportunity. She had no fear of being lonely.

13

HOW MANY MILES must Toby and Lydia have sweated, on hired bicycles, up into the foot-hills surrounding Chambérieu? They had no idea; all they knew was that they had to pedal uphill almost from the threshold of Le Grand Hôtel. Chambérieu lying in a little natural cup, each turning off the promenade tilted almost immediately: the villas lining them stepped one above the other like a flight of stairs. Most of the larger sort were *pensions,* for Chambérieu essentially lived off tourists; it was no market-town, no centre of any rich agricultural district. The cousins were in fact astonished (the last *pension* passed) to find how little the foot-hills beyond appeared to be inhabited at all. After three or four days they had interrogated no more than the same number of simple peasants— and always fruitlessly.

The more intelligent-seeming attempted to sell them wild strawberries. Toby and Lydia, who were in any case fond of wild strawberries, willingly paid their scot; but the term interrogation must apply rather to their aim than to any achievement. Lydia knew the whole of *Phèdre* by heart —it was another rôle she longed to play—and Toby could read a French railway-guide; what they lacked was any

familiarity with the local patois. Even Toby's brilliant imi-
tation of a plane going *pan, boum!* aroused less interest
than suspicion in the clear blue eyes in the blank pale faces
of the simple peasants in the foot-hills about Chambérieu.

An odd and unexpectedly disconcerting factor was the
shape of their hats. The regulation summer headgear was
evidently of straw woven into the shape of the sun-helmet,
or topee, adopted by the British while conquering India;
they made Toby feel as though he had wandered back into
the pages of Henty or Captain Brereton. In extreme youth
he had been a Henty and Brereton addict, often himself
impersonating steely-eyed District Officers; to be on the re-
ceiving-end, so to speak, of a steely eye under a sun-helmet
idiotically disconcerted him. "We're getting nowhere,"
complained Lydia. "Can't you be firmer with them?" But
what with lack of the patois, and Henty and Captain
Brereton, Toby couldn't . . .

Though neither admitted it to the other, nor indeed to
themselves, they were becoming slightly dispirited. They
still cycled into the foot-hills each morning; usually didn't
return (after a luncheon of hard-boiled eggs and, inevita-
bly, wild strawberries) until late afternoon. What made
the rest of the day so tedious was that in so small a town-
ship as Chambérieu, and one so frequented by British
visitors, the cousins couldn't fail—handsome Toby, interesting Lydia—to attract the sympathetic notice of their
compatriots. They early learnt to avoid the English Library,
wherein like a crab under a stone lurked a retired Colonel
of Sappers whose wife organized little picnics. The pro-
prietress herself (a spinster originally from Stoke-on-Trent)
gave little teas. Neither gave fun-parties, neither was in the

least degree *louche:* only inquisitive; and after their experience with Mr. Dumbly, Toby was cagey as Lydia. He hadn't been present at her single attempt to take out a novel, but he thoroughly approved her tactics.

"Actually I'm collecting Alpine flora," explained Lydia, "to press in an album to win a Duke of Edinburgh award." "Jolly good!" said the Colonel. "You must let the Mem give you a few tips." "I'm tremendously hooked on Alpines myself," declared Miss Lloyd, in her bright, slangy way. "And that good-looking boy with you?" "Actually what m' cousin's hooked on," said Lydia, in a lowered voice, "is marijuana . . ."

Either it was the disreputable truth or a piece of impertinence. Colonel McNab inclined to the first view, Miss Lloyd to the latter; in any case, Lydia was asked no more questions before she walked out empty-handed—the library affording no copy of the Kinsey Report. "*Not* very desirable young people after all," murmured Miss Lloyd. "Drugs," muttered the Colonel. "I wonder should I drop a word to old Dumbly?" "No, no," said Miss Lloyd. "The less notice taken of them the better. They should just be *ignored* . . ."

Unfortunately the Colonel's wife, a truly good W.V.S. type of woman, disagreed. Her long stag-like face alight with altruism, her long white teeth gleaming like the Hound of Heaven's (for she always travelled proper, British tooth-paste), Mrs. McNab so constantly popped up in the cousins' path, Toby and Lydia whenever they weren't cycling in the foot-hills dived into the local Cinéma des Beaux Arts showing second-run Westerns.

2.

Answering a phone call from Amsterdam, Mrs. Prelude in Buckinghamshire invited Mr. van Hoyt to tea. Most intercontinental calls prompt dinner or at least luncheon invitations: Mrs. Prelude's simple bidding to tea did her no harm with impatient Mr. van Hoyt. He was a man who liked having tea. He planned to get home to tea quite often, in that lovely home outside Boston. "I'll bake you a cake!" promised Mrs. Prelude—seldom can an intercontinental line have carried so cosily domestic a message, but involving about six million dollars. "Cherry or sultana?"

"Cherry," yearned Mr. van Hoyt. "I haven't tasted a home-baked cherry cake in years . . ."

The date was for the following Monday; ringing off, Mrs. Prelude remembered Alice due to be staying nearby, and without precisely examining her motive—when did she ever examine a motive?—dropped a note inviting Alice to tea too. Mrs. Prelude just felt it would be nice for Alice to meet Mr. van Hoyt. —For a moment she contemplated inviting Alice's father as well; but somehow had the notion that the two men mightn't get on . . .

It then struck her that it would be nice if William and Elizabeth and Lydia met him. She didn't know Mr. van Hoyt's movements; he had said something about Rome, his time in England, as before, might be counted in hours rather than days; but if he did have to go away, mightn't he *come back*, thought Mrs. Prelude daringly, for the already planned family lunch-party?

"I'll ask him when I see him," decided Mrs. Prelude.

3.

Across a dinner-table in one of the best hotels in the Lake District, Wilfred Prelude handed his wife a small chip of glistening rock. Even less than a week of holiday had put colour in his cheeks, he looked fitter altogether, for he was taking more exercise than usual, often stopping the car to scramble a quarter of a mile uphill while his wife waited below.

"Spar?" asked Mrs. Wilfred hopefully.

"I'm not sure. It might be granite with a touch of mica. Arthur would probably have known at once."

He had bought himself a small geological hammer, also a canvas bag to put specimens in.

"I'm sure that man at the chemist's could tell you, darling."

"No," said Wilfred Prelude. "When I get back I shall take them to the National Geological. Should you mind if we didn't move on for a few days? I thought of hiring a cycle."

"Of course I shouldn't," said Mrs. Wilfred.

She was in fact delighted. In previous years only perpetual motion, the magnetism of an itinerary, had kept her husband's nose to the holiday-grind; she herself often returned home quite exhausted by a succession of over-night stops. "Dear Arthur!" thought Mrs. Wilfred suddenly. She felt more than ever sure they'd misjudged him, as from beyond the grave his brotherly hand stretched forth to place Wilfred's on a handle-bar. Or so to speak.

Then she smiled amusedly.

"It seemed such an odd idea when Toby wanted to go off cycling!—and now you too! Oh, well, I suppose it's like father, like son!"

Slowly, unexpectedly, at the banal phrase, the new colour in Wilfred Prelude's cheeks deepened. He had always tended to regard Toby as more his wife's progeny than his own. It was his wife's brothers and cousins who had been to Eton: he and Arthur were strictly Grammar-school. (Unlike Arthur, Wilfred Prelude married late—his place in the new meritocracy assured.) It was from the distaff side that Toby derived his height and his handsomeness. There were moments, especially at the beginning of a vacation, when Wilfred felt himself in the presence of a courteous stranger. The words *like father, like son* warmed and stirred him. With a rare impulse he closed his hand over his wife's so firmly, the sliver of rock pricked her palm just as had the claws of Lydia's rabbits pricked the palm of William . . .

"Dear Toby, I hope he's having a gay time!" said Mrs. Wilfred, at once nervously and expectantly. "Would you like to turn in early?"

4.

In Chambérieu it was raining with a steady, even, drenching mountain rain. It had been raining all night. The tilted streets ran like gutters; under the elms of the promenade runnels from the sodden foliage collected in pools. It was far too wet to go cycling in the foot-hills, and the cinema didn't open till five. Toby and Lydia spent the afternoon in the Café des Abeilles drinking black coffee. At least in such weather there was no fear of Mrs. McNab's being abroad . . .

The little open-air colony of curly iron chairs and tables (now of course dripping like everything else) had seemed rather gay; inside, the café depressed. The general impression was of deal tarted with plastic. An eponymous plaster bee-hive needed re-touching, the proprietor a shave. Of the agile waiter there was no sign; he was probably attending his mother's funeral. Shortly after the cousins entered, a white-faced young Frenchman came in and ordered mineral-water; otherwise the place was empty.

"I dare say it's gayer at night," said Toby.

"Why?" asked Lydia.

"Well, there's a juke-box . . ."

There was also an automatic football-game—*Insert coin and turn handle*. Both centre-forwards however had run off their grooves.

Suddenly the young Frenchman sighed. It was a sigh designed to attract notice; worse, to attract sympathy. Toby and Lydia with none to spare, they were feeling too disconsolate themselves, looked hard into their coffee-cups. The young Frenchman rose and approached nonetheless, bringing his mineral-water with him, and asked if they knew Birmingham.

"No," said Toby. Lydia merely shook her head. He looked sorry for them. —But he was evidently sorrier still for himself. Uninvited, he sat; uninvited, in all too fluent English, unfolded the pathetic tale of one who after the glories of the Resistance and a glamorous spell as waiter in the Midlands was condemned for life to a one-horse town like Chambérieu. Each fresh detail was more harrowing than the last: it was the widowhood of an ailing mother that called him home—for without the pittance paid him at the Mairie, how could she live? Two elder brothers had died fighting with de Gaulle . . .

The skies without darkened before a final cloud-burst. There was a clap of thunder. The electric-light current perceptibly weakened. For a moment all was still ere the rain drummed down again.

"Chambérieu!" sighed the young Frenchman. "No theatre, no intelligentsia, nothing but old Westerns! Even the peasants are driven to invent fables, legends, to amuse themselves with . . . such as that of the rich Englishman, they say, who after a plane-crash lost his wits and exists still somewhere on the mountain . . . What a laugh!"

14

UNDER THE PLASTIC table-cloth Lydia reached for Toby's hand. His reciprocal clasp stickied both their palms.

"But it's not," said Lydia huskily. "It's not a laugh. We know. And thank heaven we've met you!"

Toby for his part swiftly ordered another mineral-water. But it wasn't only the sudden change from glum indifference to fervent welcome that surprised—for surprised indeed, and naturally, looked their new-found friend, as he mentioned that he'd prefer red wine.

"You too have heard? Even I, René Perrier, born and bred here, only yesterday picked up the gen myself. You understand the patois?"

"Never mind about that, go on," said Toby. "It's more than a fable: we have inside information."

"Forgive me if I cannot agree," smiled René Perrier. "After every such tragedy there are rumours. Our peasants are in their own way imaginative: like children, they invent stories. In this case, as I said, it is that after the crash one of the survivors, a rich Englishman, shocked and almost witless, wandered away—"

"Into the hills . . ." murmured Lydia.

"Exactly, Mademoiselle. He wandered until he dropped from exhaustion. Then someone found him, some small-holder half witless himself (they are very inbred, our mountain-people), and took him in as he would have taken in a dog. One can always do with a *coup de main*, on those small-holdings! So now, the tale goes, there is an English millionaire working with his hands for a bit of bread and sleeping in an out-house instead of at the Ritz. It is a fantasy highly pleasing to the peasant mind . . ."

Lydia could wait no longer. It was too wonderful, to have every guess so accurately confirmed.

"Do you know who that Englishman is?" she asked thrillingly. "My father! Will you come and help us look for him?"

2.

How different René Perrier from Mr. Dumbly! After only the slightest pause, instant with comfort and aid! He asked no questions, attempted no argument; simply got down to business.

"There would of course be a reward?" (As Toby subsequently remarked to Lydia, this was when he knew they could trust him. Anything in the nature of Boy-Scoutishness, in a Frenchman, would have aroused Toby's suspicion at once.) "I ask only because there has been nothing in the continental edition of *The Times*."

"The family until this moment has simply reeled under the blow," explained Toby.

"But if any help I can give should lead to the discovery of Mademoiselle's father still living—?"

"Of course there'll be a reward!" cried Lydia. "A thousand pounds!"

It was purely by chance she didn't say five, or ten, or fifty; but René seemed content.

"I must still warn you," he stated formally, "that in my opinion it is fantasy only. At the same time, such a rum do is not past belief. There are small-holdings on the mountain so remote, so difficult to find, even the tax-collector does not bother with them; the proprietors come down to market once a month with a sack of potatoes, a basket of wild strawberries, buy a little coffee, a little sugar, speak to no one, go back. They were good places for the Maquis. On such a one Mademoiselle's father might live unsuspected for donkey's years."

"That was our own idea," said Toby. "We've been looking for him, on bicycles."

"Very sensible," approved René. "No motor-car could make the grade."

"Only we haven't so far," admitted Toby, "made much headway."

René sighed understandingly. —His experience naturally didn't include the effects of too much Henty, too much Captain Brereton, on the psyche of a juvenile Anglo-Saxon male; but he understood enough.

"You speak the patois?" he asked again.

"No, but you do," said Lydia swiftly. She looked at Toby; he nodded. "Will you come with us—starting tomorrow?"

Even with a possible thousand pounds in prospect, René prudently hesitated.

"To take a day off, from the Mairie, I would lose a day's pay, Mademoiselle."

"Of course we'd make it up," said Lydia.

"There would also be expenses. I too should need to hire a bike . . . also perhaps a little in the way of bribery, to loosen a neighbour's tongue . . ."

"Of course we'd stake you," said Toby. "How much a go?"

"A fiver?" suggested René.

"To be deducted from the reward," said hard-headed Toby.

"Call it a deal," said René. "Only I had better, until I have a line, go alone. They are very suspicious, on the mountain: I as a local type could ask questions and perhaps receive answers; in the presence of strangers one and all would clam up."

Both Toby and Lydia, however reluctantly, saw the sense of this. It was agreed that René by himself should set off each day on a different trail (they were too sensible to expect immediate results), and report each evening at the Café des Abeilles.

"Only outside," added Lydia hastily, "if it isn't raining . . ."

3.

René's aid and comfort extended even further. Finishing a second carafe of red wine, which by this time the cousins also were drinking—

"Where are you putting up?" he enquired solicitously.

"At the Grand," said Toby.

René started.

"A den of thieves! Now my aunt, as it happens, runs a little *pension*—very clean, beautiful views—where you would live like fighting-cocks for the price of Le Grand Hôtel's breakfast . . ."

As Toby subsequently, additionally, pointed out to Lydia, all René's ideas were so sound. Thanks to Bobo they could afford the Grand without strain, but where was the sense in spending money at an hotel if they could put up for half the price in much more genuinely local surroundings? —There was some slight difficulty about checking out; the desk-clerk at the Grand (a den of thieves indeed) swore not only that Monsieur had definitely booked in for a month, but also that as a consequence a titled fellow-countryman had been turned away; Monsieur must naturally expect to pay a penalty? But René was there to quash this blackmail in a flood of French too rapid for the cousins to follow, and personally helped Toby repack his rucksack. —That all Lydia's possessions so easily went in too scandalized him afresh; indeed Lydia, in the hills all day and in the cinema all evening, had found time to purchase but the barest necessities. "When if there is one thing Chambérieu can offer it is undies!" exclaimed René reproachfully; and the evening, under diminishing rain, ended in a very pleasant little shopping expedition. Lydia found the exquisitely embroidered lawns and linens irresistible, however inappropriate to a cycling-tour; and René kept an eye on the saleswomen in case she was overcharged. It was a real grief to him that she needed soap: even what Chambérieu legitimately charged for the English variety (and he could honestly recommend no other) being past belief . . .

"And now for Tante Adèle's!" exclaimed René. "Where I must leave you while I nip home to my mum."

The *pension* of René's aunt turned out to be one of the smaller villas lining a tilted street; Toby and Lydia were not surprised that they never met any other guests. Immediately, however, after a brief colloquy with her nephew behind a door, Tante Adèle unlocked two small backbedrooms undoubtedly clean (if smelling slightly of mice), and the stew she served for supper was far more local than anything offered by the Grand Hôtel. —Of course at the hotel there were baths: however, René's aunt provided a can of hot water apiece for them to carry upstairs. Toby carried Lydia's for her; she was by this time so somnolent with stew and tipsy with hope, she'd have spilled every drop. Clinging to the banister starry-eyed—

"I had a sign, I didn't tell you, in that church with the *beau jubé,*" murmured Lydia. "And now what luck, what wonderful, miraculous luck, to have met René!"

4.

René's Tante Adèle always sat up late. She liked to see all her neighbours' lights out, all servant-girls—she knew each one's day off—punctually returned; not until the last dog had been exercised and the last cat called in did she quit her post at a first-floor front window. (*"Tou-Tou, Tou-Tou, Tou-Tou!"*—that was Madame Duvivier; *"Mimi, Mimi, Mimi!"*—that was Mademoiselle Agnès.) On this night, however, Tante Adèle listened, and observed, not from her window but from the stairs.

Most of what her nephew had muttered to her she simply disbelieved. Like Mrs. Armadale, she settled for an elopement: and in her way as much a voyeur as any member of the fun-party, had crept cautiously to listen first at one back-bedroom door, then at the other. —From behind neither came the slightest sound: surprised, she retreated to the stairs and sat down. The space dividing the two doors was so narrow, it could be crossed in a flash; Tante Adèle had to watch like a cat at a mousehole. For a woman past seventy the situation was tiring enough; Tante Adèle still, patiently, waited. She had often wondered (observant of silent honeymooners each engrossed in a guide-book) how the English set about getting into bed . . .

Two full hours, until midnight, waited Tante Adèle, to mark a flitting form, to hear either virginal squeak or welcoming gurgle. (*"Mimi, Mimi, Mimi? "Tou-Tou, Tou-Tou, Tou-Tou!"*) Actually both Toby and Lydia were sleeping like logs. Even in a double bed they'd have slept like logs. About midnight Tante Adèle went to bed herself.

What she missed is almost too painful to relate. Hortense, the servant-girl of Mademoiselle Agnès, returning with her fiancé in the post office, was brutally attacked by a previous (unsuspected) fiancé in the Spahis. The brave postman attacked the Spahi; Hortense attacked the postman; all three were taken in charge by the police. Tante Adèle, for once absent from her station, missed the whole drama, and had to hear about it next day from her hated neighbour Madame Duvivier.

15

NEITHER TOBY NOR LYDIA was sorry for a rest. They had been hard on the go for eight days, and after so much cycling up and down hill their leg-muscles in particular ached. (So for the matter of that did Wilfred Prelude's; but both he and his wife looked rejuvenated.) It was pleasant to idle away a morning in the *pension's* tiny back-garden desultorily cleaning their bicycles and picking cherries from an ancient cherry-tree; pleasant in the afternoon to snooze on the rough grass beneath. The weather was fine again; halcyon weather; Lydia washed her hair and dried it in the sun. A favourite topic of discussion was the exact wording of the telegram to be sent to Mrs. Prelude: they felt they ought to have it ready, so as not to waste an instant.

"Because I saw, even if William and Elizabeth wouldn't, how Mother was suffering," said Lydia. "She tried to sublimate it—isn't that Freudian too?—by cooking the most enormous meals. Her two old bids and I were simply stuffed, with fried chicken. Let's just wire FATHER FOUND, and send another longer one when we know how we'll be bringing him home."

"It may still be a bit of a shock," said Toby thoughtfully. "Better begin, GOOD NEWS."

"GOOD NEWS FATHER FOUND?"

"That seems to cover it," said Toby.

Thus the whole day built up to the moment when they met René outside the Café des Abeilles to drink red wine and hear his report. It was a moment of almost unbearable excitement, as he at last appeared—sometimes as late as eight o'clock, for he put in a long day—dusty, dog-tired, but perhaps with miraculous news . . .

Unfortunately such was never the case. To whatever remote fastnesses he had penetrated, however many small-holders he'd bribed, René drew blank. He himself admitted as surprising the number of hermits, and even fugitives from justice, he'd flushed: but not one by any possibility Mr. Prelude. Yet it was obvious that he had begun to come round to the cousins' opinion; why else, unless one of their number had found unpaid labour, should simple peasants at the chatty mention of a popular rumour so instantly clam up? Pocketing each fresh fiver (hard-headed Toby was paying by the day), René bade Mademoiselle still hope . . .

It was wonderfully exciting and agreeable, under the elms of the promenade. The fairy-lights overhead lent an air of festivity and romance; as René practically sweated into his wine-glass—though pale, he was of full habit— Lydia and Toby felt bound in such sympathy with their French comrade, they felt like two of the Three Muske-teers. —Neither would have admitted it, Dumas like Henty and Captain Brereton belonging to childhood; but Lydia mentally rehearsed the rôle of Aramis *en travesti*. They didn't talk much; just sat tipping back their chairs, sipping red wine, watching an occasional fairy-light fuse.

No less was René touched by the poetry of the situation. After his spell in Birmingham, after (to be frank) certain snubbings by Anglo-Saxon tourists, to sit under the elms in company with high-class British pals impinged on his sensibilities like a verse of Lamartine.

"Nice, ain't it?" offered René.

"Nice," echoed Lydia.

Toby momentarily abandoned the role of Porthos to nod agreement. It was nice indeed, sitting under the elms, sipping red wine, watching the fairy-lights fuse. After these had been officially switched off René saw his pals home. Sometimes they sang "Alouette," sometimes "Frère Jacques"; and that was nice too.

2.

"Of course I never intended to be home," said Elizabeth, stretched on the Grecian shore, "for another ghastly family lunch. But Mother says she's asking Mr. van Hoyt. She thinks it would be nice for us children to meet Father's oldest friend."

Henry raised his eyebrows. —They had bleached as his skin tanned; as fair as Elizabeth was dark, he had developed a rather Scandinavian look which made him by no means less attractive to the gigolo-toting promenaders.

"Oh, I agree," said Elizabeth. "One has to know Mother, to realize that's exactly all she genuinely thinks she thinks. The danger as I see it is if he jumps the gun she'll start having scruples about Father not cold in the grave . . . I could always fly over and fly back."

"Leaving me locked in an hotel bed-room?" suggested Henry Alcott.

Elizabeth was sufficiently struck to sit up and pull off her sun-glasses.

"Am I showing signs of possessiveness?"

"Definitely," said Henry. "I don't mind. In fact I think it may be rather a good opportunity for me to meet the family myself. Did you know your eyes changed colour? Usually they're grey; now they're quite blue."

"Many a man has noticed sooner," said Elizabeth.

"I hope less distracted by your thighs," said Henry. "We'll both fly over and fly back."

3.

The cousins had still every confidence in their French comrade; but time was passing. Thursday, Friday, Saturday and Sunday had passed, fruitless save of renewed hope. ("A potato-patch newly hoed!" reported René. "Wild strawberries gathered high up! By whom? Maybe Mademoiselle's dad!") Lydia and Toby still so trusted him, it was chiefly because they'd found their legs again, because they were rested and inactivity had begun to bore, that on the Monday they insisted on joining the foray themselves.

René did his best to dissuade, re-employing all his original arguments; but Lydia and Toby promised at the first sign of a likely small-holding to cycle swiftly on as though having no connection. "It may not be possible at this season to hire bikes," warned René. "I myself had to bribe a little . . ." "But we've got 'em," said Toby. "They're in your aunt's shed." "You mean you have been paying through the nose while they lay idle?" exclaimed René. "We hired 'em for a fortnight," explained Toby, "payment in advance." "If you had told me," sighed René, "I might have made a deal for you . . ." He sighed again; shrugged. For a moment, in the face of such irrational obstinacy —("One boob, and all my spade-work hit for six!")—he appeared to contemplate throwing in his hand and letting the cousins set out alone. But loyalty, however mixed with disapproval, won. "You will at least see some country," promised René cynically, "before we all three hang-dog return!"

Actually the machines hired by Toby and Lydia, compared with René's, were rather inferior—one a low-handled racing-type but with a loose chain, the other designed for a lady to sit peculiarly upright upon; both in horse-coper parlance aged. René's own mount was rather showily chromium-plated and had a three-speed gear. Neither Lydia nor Toby begrudged it him, however, when they thought of how many uphill miles he'd already altruistically cycled: as they strung out behind him—Lydia in the middle, Toby in the rear—only their sense of gratitude equalled their sense of adventure.

4.

"Where are we going?" called Lydia, pedalling through a hamlet apparently composed of a church and a post office.

"Somewhere not far," reassured René. "Remote only because the road is so bad . . ."

The road was certainly bad enough, after they almost immediately turned aside and began to pedal uphill. Soon it was no more than a track: pebbles sprayed from beneath their wheels, on either side a low encroaching undergrowth tangled with the spokes. As the morning warmed up René began to sweat heavily; Toby and Lydia, lighter-boned and far less fully fleshed, could have overtaken him easily, had the path been wide enough and if he hadn't been their guide.

"What's the place called?" shouted Toby from the rear.

"It has not even a name," panted René. "It is too remote and tatty . . ."

"Just where Father might *be!*" breathed Lydia.

Onwards and upwards the comrades pedalled, René with his head bowed over his handle-bars looking neither to left nor right, Toby and Lydia glancing interestedly about them. —It was actually the latter who as the bushes on one side rose and levelled to a rough hedge spotted the hurdle roughly doing duty as a gate.

"We're by some sort of tatty place now," called Lydia. "Oughtn't we to stop?"

"If we stop at every dung-heap on the way," panted René, "night will fall!"

He pedalled on. But Toby too had dismounted. René, again recognizing an insular stubbornness, resignedly followed suit and wheeled his bicycle back. However, as all three leaned and looked over the hurdle, the half-acre immediately before them stretched so obviously uncultivated, so rank with weeds and thistly, his guess that no one lived there at all made sense.

"One sees only too many such abandoned properties," lamented René. "Industrialization the ruin of the country! Now that Mademoiselle is content—"

"Yes, but on the other side there's wire," said Lydia. "Wire netting."

"To keep rabbits out," said Toby.

"So something's being grown; so someone's there . . ."

"Maybe an old woman hoeing potatoes," scoffed René.

"Did *you* see someone? I did too," said Lydia.

Completely forgetting the promise to leave René unhampered, she surmounted the hurdle with agile ease. So did Toby. René—("We are in any case trespassing!" he warned)—took time to unfasten a withy. But all three were more or less together as they hastened across abandoned ridge-and-furrow towards the wire fence: on the other side of which, in precisely the attitude Lydia had pictured, not an old woman but an old man looked up startled from his hoe.

16

H E WORE A PAIR of black cloth trousers and a peasant's blouse, both garments much patched, also so
far too large they hung like the clothes on a scarecrow. All
that could be distinguished of his frame was that it was
spare and below medium height. A rough-cut fringe of
greying hair and a full greying beard masked his features
as effectively as any mask specially imported for a fun-party;
over all—face, hair, raiment—a light powdering of dust
further obliterated any characteristic whether of quality of
cloth or set of eye-socket. For a moment, anonymous and
indigenous-appearing as a thistle, he stood a-stare; then with
shambling steps turned and made for the open door of a
low, semi-derelict shed.

Lydia moved first: catching up with him on its threshold
was just in time, as he let fall his hoe, to support him under
the lintel into the circumscribed coolth and darkness
within. —One instant he staggered, the next was hanging
upon her neck racked by a bout of asthmatical coughing—
how familiar to Lydia the harrowing sound!—that seemed
to shake the last of his strength out of him. He was
speechless; barely, it seemed, conscious. One dusty hand

still momentarily unclasped; hesitantly, very gently, he stroked Lydia's cheek . . .

He was in tears.

"Father!" cried Lydia. " 'Tis I, Lydia, your child!"

2.

Behind her she heard Toby's gasp, René's exclamation. It was well they had followed: though pitiably light, the burden was too much for her to support alone. "Hold up, sir!" adjured Toby, pulling a blue-bloused sleeve across his shoulder. But the knees in the dusty black trousers had buckled irretrievably. They had to heave him up as they'd had to heave up Mrs. Armadale; were glad of René's help. "We must get him somewhere where he can lie down," panted Lydia. "Where's the house?" "Too far," panted René. "Lay him down where he is!"

A rough pallet indeed the shed offered, of sheepskins over straw. ("Where he's been *sleeping!*" thought Lydia, indignation mingling with pity, and wonder with both; it was quite miraculous how every detail of her prevision was coming true.) Gently, between them, they laid their unconscious burden down: Lydia, remembering how her father when recumbent needed to have his head and chest propped up, heaped the straw higher at one end. It wasn't the special anti-asthma pillow Mrs. Prelude travelled, but an unconscious sigh accepted it gratefully.

"Poor Father!" mourned Lydia. "Darling Dad! —Toby, bike back to that post office and send the wire!"

3.

Off raced Toby to the gap. In the shed Lydia crouched close beside the pallet; René, probably from delicacy, withdrew to lean under the lintel. It was so low, he had to duck every time he shifted stance; and though aware of him but as an uneasy presence, because she remembered how much they owed him—

"Don't mind coming in," said Lydia. "Sit down on something. It may be quite a long time before Father can talk . . ."

René ducked again and found a sack of potatoes. It was a come-anything-going sort of shed; Lydia found herself crouched on an old bee-hive. It placed her at exactly the right level, however, to sit and hold one of the toil-worn hands.

All was very quiet, in the shed. No angry small-holder irrupted to threaten with a discarded hoe. It was as quiet as in a moon-lit orchard in Buckinghamshire; almost (the shed having no windows) as dark. Even with the door open, all René could discern was a vague tableau as of King Lear watched over by Cordelia. It was still a tear-jerker. As above the two clasped hands—the one so young and smooth, the other so old and horny—sleek black locks drooped to mingle with a greying beard, René blinked. —He blinked, he looked away; looked back and blinked again. In short, he was so powerfully affected, he could no longer keep silence.

"Mademoiselle," said René huskily.

[*140*]

4.

Lydia half-turned.

"Hasn't Toby been gone *ages?*"

"If he was a giddy goat, he could not be back yet," said René. "Mademoiselle—"

"I should have told him to get a car. Or an ambulance."

"Mademoiselle, please hear me," said René. "I have something on my chest."

He paused; Lydia, now that she took a look at him, saw the emotion in his voice reflected on his face. It crossed her mind that he was about to tell her he was in love with her: she quickly, instinctively shook her head. But as René drew painful breath his expression from wretched became so guilty, with a slight sense of disappointment (irrational but natural) Lydia changed her mind and prepared for the admission that he'd never been with the Maquis after all. Again, she erred.

"When I first strung along with you," pronounced René, "I did not for two shakes believe your dad still in the land of the living."

"But I know," said Lydia, surprised. "Didn't you warn us that the rumour might be only a rumour?"

René shook his miserable head.

"There was no rumour. It was an invention. Cooked up. My cousin, Mademoiselle, was in the outer office when you came in your distress to Mr. Dumbly. We split fifty-fifty."

"I simply don't understand what you're talking about," said Lydia.

"He listened," explained René patiently. "It is not what you would do, but it is what Jean did. He was in agreement with Mr. Dumbly. But he saw also the possibilities, but for the fear that you might remember him and smell rats he would have played the comedy himself. That is where I came in . . ."

There was a long pause. No more than William or Elizabeth did Lydia easily suspect mercenariness; she needed time to comprehend. —The figure on the pallet stirred; with her free hand she pulled straw up higher, smoothed a lap of sheepskin, before she spoke again.

"Then I think," she said slowly, "that's the meanest thing I ever heard."

"Yes, Mademoiselle. It was very mean."

"I still don't see why. To think Father would never be found meant you couldn't think there'd be a reward."

"No, but there were the fivers," explained René. "Your fivers every time I took a day off. I did not even look for your dad. This morning, because you were with me, is the first time I have been farther than my mum's allotment. She grows asparagus for the Grand Hotel."

More than ever Lydia wished Toby back, to give their false friend a dressing-down in stronger terms than she herself could command. But feeling the clasp on her wrist moment by moment increase in strength, how could she not forgive?

"After all," meditated Lydia, "it is in a way owing to you that Father's been found . . ."

To her renewed surprise, René wrung his hands. (A gesture she'd frequently seen performed upon the stage, but never in real life; even at such a juncture, she noticed that stage-elbows jerked too high.)

"But he has not!" cried René desperately. "It is all an error! That is no more your parent than he is General de Gaulle!"

It was quite unconsciously that Lydia released herself; simply to confront him more directly.

"If you imagine I can't recognize my own father—" she began hotly.

"I do not imagine, I know," said René. "Naturally you deceived yourself: over-emotional, predisposed—how naturally! But the farce has gone far enough, now I am ashamed of my part in it, in time I will try to pay your fivers back. Mademoiselle: that is not your dad, he cannot be your dad, for the reason that he is my Uncle Marius a little weak in the head whom I have known since I was four years old. If you wish to see, there are all his papers in my Tante Eugénie's dresser-drawer up at the house."

It is always hard, to the young it is almost impossible, to find a dream realized still no more than a dream.

"You lied before," said Lydia. "You've just admitted it. And don't you forget something? *He* recognized me."

"If you mean he caressed you, any woman a little kind to him he caresses," said René harshly. "It is his way, we are used to them, his foolish tears and caresses! And though I have lied before, why should I now, to my disadvantage? You yourself cannot pay the reward and your elders would not be deceived; but how many fivers more, just to buy clothes for the old fool? Except that I am as I say ashamed, having taken advantage of such innocence."

Lydia stared.

[143]

"Innocence?" she repeated incredulously. "Toby and I *innocents?*"

"As babes, Mademoiselle. As my Tante Adèle says, *Paul et Virginie!* —Think, Mademoiselle, for God's sake think!" implored René. "If you will not take my word, is there no single physical point by which your dad can be identified beyond doubt?"

"Of course," said Lydia bravely. "His teeth. I thought of that at home straight away. But it needs Mr. Hambury-White."

"His own teeth?" asked René quickly.

"Yes."

With a gesture of some crudity René yanked apart the ancient's jaws (much as he'd have yanked apart the jaws of an old horse), yanked out upper and lower plate. The gums thus revealed were blackish and hard as iron. Mr. Hambury-White would have shuddered at the sight of them. —So did Lydia shudder, and burst into tears.

5.

At which moment Toby panted back out of breath but triumphant.

"It's off!" he reported gladly. "I had the deuce of a time spelling out Buckinghamshire—B for Boutique, U for Ursulines, C for Camembert—but I've sent it!"

To his surprise, his cousin turned on him a look of blankest dismay; neither she nor René seemed capable of speech. —Toby cast an anxious glance towards the pallet;

had his uncle finally passed out? But a slight asthmatic snort reassured . . .

"I'm terribly sorry," said Lydia, "but we'd better wire again."

"Saying what?" demanded Toby.

"ALL A TERRIBLE MISTAKE," said Lydia.

17

NOT UNCOMMONLY two cables dispatched from France to England within an hour of each other arrive at the same time. In this instance, however, Toby's first had the field to itself, whereas the second tangled with a flock of congratulations from local vignerons to their Deputy in Paris on the occasion of his magnificent speech in favour of wine versus Coca-Cola. The postmistress had no doubt as to priorities: every single inland telegram was sent off—(some saying no more than "*Bravo, M. Dupont!*"; others thirty words long)—before she spelt out Buckinghamshire again, and at about two o'clock Mrs. Prelude was gladdened by Toby's first first, and solo.

She had sat up too often, in her half of a double bed, asking herself whether she had really been sure, to doubt its validity. Like Lydia, she was predisposed to belief; also neither William nor Elizabeth was at hand to inject any antidote of scepticism. Mrs. Prelude indeed tried to telephone William in London, but when there was no immediate answer (that is, after two rings), dropped the receiver at once. Perhaps her subconscious didn't want any note of scepticism? It was the fact that for a woman so accustomed, in any unusual circumstance, to lean on the advice of others, Mrs. Prelude at this really breath-taking juncture behaved with remarkable independence. She told herself that since both William and Elizabeth would be home for lunch on Thursday in any case, it would be much nicer—*fairer*—to break the glad news to both together and see their faces light. She was being so particularly level-headed, she didn't bank on their resurrected parent's being there as well—she didn't know how Lydia and Toby were bringing him, and perhaps Arthur wouldn't care to fly—but if he *were*, not only what glad news, but what glad surprise awaited! No one suspected that it was from her mother that Lydia inherited her sense of drama; but it was, and if Mrs. Prelude hadn't known the Wilfreds to be still mobile in the Lake District, she probably wouldn't even have performed the obvious, imperative duty of telephoning her brother-in-law's house. After receiving the expected answer, and leaving a reminder about Thursday lunch—it was obviously impossible to transmit such news through an Italian butler—Mrs. Prelude could give joy full rein with no more jarring note than a lobster in the refrigerator. How glad she was now that she hadn't let William instal a barrel of oysters feeding on bran in the cellar! The lobster could be buried quite easily. —When she had a moment to think, she was glad of Miss Champney's and Barbara's absence too. It wasn't that she felt guilty, about having old friends to stay, or eating shellfish: she just felt Arthur would enjoy his home-coming more thoroughly without such evidences that everyone had believed him dead. Joyfully, untroubled by any prick of conscience, undamped by any word of sense, Mrs. Prelude reassembled the inhaling-apparatus, plumped and aired the anti-asthma pillow, and reread her telegram till it wore in two.

"The good, clever children!" murmured Mrs. Prelude. —Was it chance, she wondered, or had they actually set out in search? She thought perhaps they had. She seemed to remember Lydia (alone of her offspring), not trying to argue but suggesting something helpful: like monks. "Perhaps in a monastery?" thought Mrs. Prelude. "How wrong and weak I was, not to go back myself! Dear Arthur, how I've missed you!"

She believed it without the slightest effort. Certainly her present happiness was genuine. Old friends and shellfish and Chablis are all very well, but still peanuts, to any truly womanly woman, compared with being a wife rather than a widow. "I shall have learnt to value him more than ever," Mrs. Prelude told herself. (Actually the worst dereliction she could have thought of was the umbrella incident at The Hague; but then she was less thinking than feeling.) "I'll be able to *show* him," added Mrs. Prelude, with some incoherence. "What a lucky woman I am!"

Where she was truly lucky was in the fact that with Toby's second cable still imminent, she hadn't loosed such a cat among the pigeons—in the world of international finance, besides in the family—as would be troublesome indeed to catch again. There were no headlines. (It never even occurred to her to inform the Press.) Totally unadvised, thanks to her subconscious and a sense of drama Mrs. Prelude behaved as wisely as possible. So far, no damage was done. Alice didn't turn up until nearly four.

2.

"Darling!" exclaimed Alice, jumping out of the jeep and kissing her prospective mother-in-law with enthusiasm. "How happy and excited you look!"

Mrs. Prelude started. Then she doubly controlled both her expression and her impulses. For though she wasn't expecting Alice, to be embraced by a creature so pretty and sparkling and loving—to get a good hug, in fact—seemed suddenly just what she wanted. Kissing Alice back, Mrs. Prelude achieved a slight frown; but at the same moment was tempted to break the glad news there and then and be hugged again. Why not? Alice was so nearly one of the family! Only it still wouldn't be fair, recollected Mrs. Prelude, before William and Elizabeth knew; so the moment of danger passed.

"And no wonder!" added Alice.

Mrs. Prelude more than started, she almost jumped, as for another moment she asked herself whether the child could possibly know already. But obviously she couldn't know. It was out of the question—for why should Toby and Lydia have telegraphed Alice?

"'No wonder'?" repeated Mrs. Prelude, she hoped casually.

"Well, isn't Mr. van Hoyt coming?" prompted Alice. "You asked me to meet him."

3.

Mrs. Prelude had forgotten. It wasn't surprising. When she should have been baking a cherry-cake she was reassembling Arthur's inhaling-apparatus. Mr. van Hoyt, until two o'clock figuring rather prominently in her mind, by five past had simply dropped, so to speak, through a mental oubliette. Naturally she had forgotten that she was expecting Alice as well; she had forgotten everything. —She was appalled. She also blamed herself really dreadfully; although, as Elizabeth suspected, any intimations of her own concerning Mr. van Hoyt were far less precise than his concerning her, she couldn't but recognize (in a general sort of way) that his visit was now going to be waste of time for him. In fact, when she thought (rather less generally) of what might have happened if the telegram hadn't arrived first, she turned so pale, Alice took it as a touching sign of romantic sensibility in the middle-aged.

"Thank goodness you reminded me!" exclaimed Mrs. Prelude, pulling herself together. "Oh, dear! I suppose it's too late to put him off?"

"Darling, don't be ridiculous," said Alice kindly. "We all know how much you like him."

"Of course I do," said Mrs. Prelude, in growing agitation. "That's what makes it all the worse. I could have *written* quite easily . . . But whatever are we talking about?" she added hypocritically. "He's just coming to tea, I can't put him off, I just hope he won't stay very long because I've a great deal to do. Dear Alice, as you'll be here as well—"

But Alice was a girl who always liked to get things straight, especially where millionaires in the family were concerned.

"You mean," she asked, incredulously, "if he asks you to marry him you won't? When William's all for it too?"

"I can't think what all you children have been imagining!" exclaimed Mrs. Prelude. "There's no question of my marrying anyone!" (Had Alice been less perturbed, she might have noted a missing phrase: *my dear husband scarcely cold in the grave.*) "What I was going to say was that as you'll be here as well—"

"Not I," said Alice sincerely, "I couldn't bear it."

"—you could help me by making an early move."

Alice however still refused her countenance, and Mrs. Prelude could only invite her to Thursday lunch before like a scalded little cat Alice pounced back into the jeep and censoriously drove away again; and some ten or fifteen minutes later a hired, chauffeur-driven Rolls deposited Mr. van Hoyt.

Which was when the damage was done.

4.

Not that Mrs. Prelude told, even to her husband's closest colleague. It was part of her trouble: she'd have enjoyed telling Mr. van Hoyt even more than she'd have enjoyed telling Alice—for how *his* face would light, knowing Arthur revivified to slay the French again! But loyalty to William and Elizabeth and the Wilfreds tied her tongue, and since at the same time she felt that if he really did propose the only possible ground for refusal was that she wasn't a widow after all, her every effort had to be directed at preventing a declaration. (Mrs. Prelude never ceased to admire the gallantry of males who with so much to offer, still laid themselves open to be rebuffed. "How they *can!*" thought Mrs. Prelude—her woolly but compassionate mind embracing at once the men who proposed and the women who rejected them.) "I must discourage him at once," determined Mrs. Prelude, "*hard . . .*"

Thus it was a very different woman indeed from the amiable hostess of his recollections who off-handedly greeted Mr. van Hoyt with the frank admission that she'd forgotten all about him. "I meant to bake you a cake," said Mrs. Prelude, still rather off-handedly. "I'd hoped you would," said Mr. van Hoyt. "Cherry." "Only I forgot," said Mrs. Prelude.

She didn't so much as toss him off a hot scone. All there was to eat were a few meat paste sandwiches. Not that Mr. van Hoyt had much appetite, faced by an absolute lack of interest in his new Jaeger pyjamas.

"I took your advice," reminded Mr. van Hoyt.

"William always says he wouldn't be seen dead in them," observed Mrs. Prelude absently. "Do excuse me while I telephone . . ."

She hadn't yet ordered a supply of yoghurt. She did so now, at some length, and returned carrying a parish magazine which she kept on her lap. "We've a very active church-membership in my own little community," offered Mr. van Hoyt—hoping thus to lead the conversation, if deviously,

to his swimming-pool and woodland walks. "Outside Boston," he reminded. "I thought you lived in New York?"
said cruel Mrs. Prelude. (But cruel only to be kind. It really
distressed her so to ill-treat the poor man—yet his whole
attitude, every word he spoke, warned her that Alice and
the children had been right, and that unless very firmly
discouraged indeed the declaration she so much wished to
avoid was about to be dumped in her lap alongside the
parish magazine.) "Boston," corrected Mr. van Hoyt. "All
those Irish?" said Mrs. Prelude intelligently. "I remember
Arthur once telling me he couldn't cross the street because
of a St. Patrick's Day parade." "In New York," said Mr.
van Hoyt. "That's what I *thought*," said Mrs. Prelude.
"Would you excuse me if I telephoned again?"

Like most women unused to playing a part, when she did
she rather hammed it. Scarcely had she returned when she
remembered another call to be made: her exits and re-
entries (especially as Mr. van Hoyt was a man who always
rose to his feet when his hostess did) began to introduce a
touch of farce. But at least Mr. van Hoyt was discouraged.
On her third re-entry (with a mending-basket), he didn't
sit down again.

"I guess I'm in your way," stated Mr. van Hoyt.

He paused. —So did Mrs. Prelude. For a moment she
felt so sorry for him, and so fond of him, the glad news
almost burst from her lips. But she remembered William
and Elizabeth and the Wilfreds and Alice.

"I *have*," apologized Mrs. Prelude, "a rather busy
day . . ."

"I'd hoped," said Mr. van Hoyt simply—not even reproachfully. For all his millions, his was a humble heart.

[153]

"After my recent troubles, I'd caught a glimpse of blue sky. But I guess I was mistaken."

"I'm afraid you were," said Mrs. Prelude.

"Now the clouds roll over again."

"They'll soon part," promised Mrs. Prelude—really in need of comfort herself.

"Not for me," stated Mr. van Hoyt. "God bless you all the same . . ."

He kissed her hand and went out into the night.

5.

Only of course it wasn't night. It was about half-past five on a summer afternoon. Also hobbling to any heroic departure was the circumstance that he'd liberated the chauffeur of the hired Rolls to go and get his own tea. For some moments after the door closed behind him Mr. van Hoyt stood at a loss, wondering what on earth to do with himself—where to conceal himself—until that chauffeur reappeared; and was still standing so uneasily when towards him up the short drive pattered Alice, who actually hadn't driven her jeep very far.

Mr. van Hoyt had no idea that he beheld one who might have been his daughter-in-law by marriage. He had never heard of Alice. All Mr. van Hoyt beheld (Alice halting in surprise, Alice in a white linen dress, sleek fair tresses brushing her shoulders and cheeks flushed to a rosy glow) was a creature as young and pretty and bewitching as Corinna when he first fell in love with her.

Some men never learn. He'd known how to prize a Mrs.

Prelude, but now all that was washed up, and as the memory of Corinna's charm suddenly flooded back, so did the memory of her inadequacies vanish. Recalling her curled like a sleepy, silken kitten, Mr. van Hoyt forgot that it was he who had been doing the packing. He forgot his annoyance at being referred to as the Prof, and how even during his own after-dinner speeches Corinna continued flirting with a neighbour. He forgot everything except what he'd lost in the way of youth and prettiness and gaiety— and now here before him stood all three personified . . .

Not only youth falls in love at first sight. Middle age is often hit much harder—not as by a moonbeam, rather as by a tile blown off a roof. Mr. van Hoyt still kept his moral head sufficiently to glance at the vision's left hand. It was bare. (Alice often slipped off her engagement-ring while driving, and had done so now.) She for her part returned his gaze with innocent curiosity.

"Who are you? I'm Alice," said Alice shyly.

"James van Hoyt," yearned Mr. van Hoyt.

As though emboldened by so civil an answer, she approached nearer.

"Mr. van Hoyt? Then I know *all* about you. I'm a *great friend of the family* myself," said Alice, with childlike solemnity. "Have you been to see darling Mrs. Prelude now?"

Mr. van Hoyt nodded—so dejectedly, it was plain that darling Mrs. Prelude had been as good as her word.

"So have I," said Alice, "but she didn't seem to want me. Only I left my scarf."

"I guess my own call was mistimed too," said Mr. van Hoyt. "To be frank—" with a wry gesture he indicated the empty car—"I stayed less long than I anticipated. Where would you suppose a chauffeur gets his tea, in this vicinity?"

Alice considered.

"The nearest Caff's about half-a-mile off: if he's gone on his legs he won't be back for ages. What a shame," added Alice—tactfully ambiguous as to where the blame lay, between the chauffeur and Mrs. Prelude—"when you've probably flown from somewhere!"

"Actually Rome," said Mr. van Hoyt.

Alice's eyes widened. (It was a trick William knew well: Alice with her eyes wide looked like a kitten and an orphan and a pin-up all in one.)

"The Eternal City," glossed Mr. van Hoyt. "You know it?"

"I don't know anywhere," confessed Alice. "I just stay home looking after my daddy. But to have to wait about after *Rome*—!"

Suddenly she looked diffident. (William knew that look too, and always braced himself.)

"Never mind my old scarf," said Alice, "and even if after Rome it sounds futile, would you like me to show you, while you *do* have to wait, a rather lovely woodland walk?"

Hoist with his own petard, Mr. van Hoyt followed.

6.

The path, through a spinney situated no further than the opposite side of the main road, was basically far less wild than his New England woodland walk, but at the same time less well maintained—blackberry-trails and suckers impeding every step. Alice stumbled almost immediately. As he caught and supported her the thought indeed crossed Mr. van Hoyt's mind that perhaps he needn't have flown Mrs. Prelude to Boston after all. But since that was all washed up, he had no hesitation in prolonging the contact as soft and silky as a kitten—or as Corinna—Alice nestled and took breath.

"I've such silly ankles!" apologized Alice. "Like a fairy's," said Mr. van Hoyt. "You'd better take my arm . . ."

In a small clearing, some few moments after they strayed on again, they passed a jeep. Mr. van Hoyt cast an almost sentimental glance towards it. He'd driven a jeep himself, in France, in '44: to come across one still unscrapped obscurely touched him. That Alice led on without remark touched him too. "Good grief, she doesn't even remember the war, she wasn't born!" thought Mr. van Hoyt. If this reflection rather pointed the disparity in their ages, Mr. van Hoyt overlooked it. He just felt glad that should the subject ever arise he had a Good Conduct Medal to show, in proof of manlihood. Corinna rather made fun of his medal, once she used it as an ante at poker; but no British girl would, thought Mr. van Hoyt . . .

At which point in his meditations (the jeep out of sight), Alice came clean.

"You're so nice, I've got to 'fess," choked Alice—halting so abruptly she almost stumbled again. "Though you'll probably *despise* me . . ."

"I doubt it," said Mr. van Hoyt, at once surprised, amused and tender.

"Very well, then : *I picked you up*. Isn't that awful?"

[157]

A more experienced millionaire would have thought it only natural. But Mr. van Hoyt had never been much on the town. Corinna and the call of patriotism apart, not a hairsbreadth had he strayed since leaving college from the strict paths of international banking. So he just pressed Alice's hand reassuringly until she felt better.

"Only what I hope may make you think me not *quite* so awful," continued Alice, "is *why*. I don't live here, you see, I'm just staying. I live with my daddy at Oxford. And I'm going back this evening. And the person who's going to drive me is someone I particularly don't want to be driven by—anyway not thirty miles . . . Oh, dear, how complicated it sounds—and *silly!*—when I *say* it!"

Mr. van Hoyt however was able to assimilate far more complex situations without the least difficulty, nor did he think Alice silly at all. Corinna had often raised his hair with tales of car-driving wolves—how they ran out of petrol in lonely places, or drove up to hotels and produced wedding-rings from waistcoat-pockets. He thought Alice showed great sense—not least (and how flatteringly!) in turning to himself for protection. To help her on—

"I guess it wasn't so much me you picked up, young lady," accused Mr. van Hoyt, with mock severity, "as my car."

Alice heaved a sigh of relief.

"Well, yes," she admitted frankly. "As soon as I knew who you were, *and* when I saw your car, I suddenly had this crazy idea you might drive me instead; and that's why I offered to take you for a walk. Oh, dear! Now I feel better."

"Confession is good for the soul," agreed Mr. van Hoyt.

"I still see no reason why *I* shouldn't take *you* for a ride."

He thought he put it rather wittily; indeed Alice giggled. "You will, really and truly?"

"Cross my heart," said Mr. van Hoyt—he was already feeling years younger.

"Then I'll tell you what we'll do," said Alice. "I'll wait by the road while you go to the car, and as soon as the chauffeur's back come and get me. Then we'll drive to where I'm staying and pick up my things and I'll say—I'll say—"

"You've met up with an old friend of the family," prompted Mr. van Hoyt.

"Well, you almost are, aren't you?" agreed Alice. "I mean, being such a great friend of Mrs. Prelude's, and I am too?"

To terminate at five minutes' notice a visit expected to be at least several more days, Alice simply left Mr. van Hoyt outside and informed her hostess that having been worried about Daddy's cough all along, and having met a friend of his at Mrs. Prelude's who was driving to Oxford anyway, she felt she ought to run off. "Especially as something's gone wrong with my jeep," added Alice. "I've had to leave it at Chesham." —A helpful circumstance, preventive of awkward questions, was that her hostess was rather pleased to be rid of Alice; she considered Alice a baggage—officially engaged to one man, but all too ready to encourage the attentions of any other. (The any other, in this case, the son of the house: a diffident, sensitive quantity-surveyor who never took a car out without seeing the tank full first. But he was certainly fond of driving Alice about.)

"Say good-bye to Bobby for me!" begged Alice. Her hostess readily promised; and Alice so swiftly crammed a suitcase, the Rolls was well on the way to Oxford before Mrs. Prelude received Toby's second cable, ALL A TERRIBLE MISTAKE.

18

AGAIN, SHE BELIEVED. Perhaps her subconscious had acted less to shield the flame of hope than to issue warnings—for had she truly tried to contact William or the Wilfreds? In any case, however bitterly she wept, Mrs. Prelude believed, and though through streaming tears unhesitatingly dismantled the inhaling-apparatus. "The poor children!" thought Mrs. Prelude. "What must *they* be feeling? Perhaps some heartless person deceived them; perhaps took Lydia into some hospital where she was too frightened, just as I was, to really look . . . She had a hundred pounds," thought Mrs. Prelude, with one of her rare acknowledgments of the world's wickedness. "Poor Lydia!"

Hot tears—now for Lydia too—dropped afresh upon the anti-asthma pillow, it was in a voice choked by sobs that Mrs. Prelude countermanded yoghurt; but after some hours of distressful activity she was sufficiently composed to telephone Claridge's and enquire whether Mr. van Hoyt was as usual staying there, and if so, till when.

—"Don't page him," added Mrs. Prelude hastily. "Unless he's just checking out . . ."

She felt it would be less embarrassing on both sides to

make her apologies by letter. For of course she had to apologize. The memory of how she'd mistreated the poor man was by now almost her worst affliction. She had been unkind, she had been inhospitable, she had been downright rude. Even had Mr. van Hoyt been no more than a casual acquaintance, it was her plain duty as a gentlewoman to apologize to him; and learning that his room was booked for a week, she sat down at her desk feeling better already.

> DEAR FRIEND [wrote Mrs. Prelude],
> *If I was horrid this afternoon, as I know I was, it was because I had just received some very unexpected family news very much on my mind. But now it's all smoothed out —*

Here she paused. The moderation of her opening had been deliberate—since she obviously couldn't go into details; but did she really mean *smoothed out?* The words seemed to have written themselves. However, once down in black and white they had such a look of inevitability, she let them stand.

> *— and I really am glad you went to Jaegers. So please do if you can come and see me again before you leave Europe. Next Thursday for lunch would be perfect, for then you could meet the children, as I want you to very much.*
>> *Believe me, most sincerely,*
>>> MARY PRELUDE
> *Have the clouds rolled away just a little?*

2.

The letter posted, Mrs. Prelude once again did the most sensible thing possible: she went to bed. All alone in the house, she made herself as comfortable as if she'd been under observation in a fashionable clinic. —Possibly more so; the clinic mightn't have allowed lobster. Mrs. Prelude first cleft and chipped at the rosy carapace, also mixed a nice little salad, drew the cork from a half-bottle of Chablis, and set all out on a tray. Then she took a hot bath and had supper in bed. Not once all night, despite the lobster, did she either dream or rouse; but she must have stirred, for having dropped off as usual on her own side of the double bed, when she woke in the morning she was in the middle.

The third telegram from Lydia and Toby arrived soon after breakfast.

19

THEY HAD SAT to compose it, the previous evening, at their usual table under the elms across the road from the Café des Abeilles. Only this time they weren't waiting for René. Nor were they drinking red wine, but tea and *citron pressé*. Lydia had wept so much, and Toby had cycled up and down hill so much, they were too thirsty to bother about being sophisticated. It marked perhaps a stage in their education.

"But why wire your lot at all?" objected Lydia—for such to begin with was Toby's intention. "If Mother's told about our first she'll have told about our other. I mean, don't let's make a *thing* of it."

It was a comfort to both of them to think that Mrs. Prelude's hopes couldn't have been long raised before they were dashed again. As Toby knowledgeably pointed out, two telegrams dispatched from France to England within an hour of each other might even arrive at the same time; it just depended on which Mrs. Prelude opened first whether she'd had her hopes raised at all . . .

"Anyway you don't know where they are," added Lydia. "You can't just put WILFRED PRELUDES, LAKE DISTRICT."

"M' dad telephones home each night," said Toby. "You can't think I want to, can you?"

"Then it's sheer masochism. If Mother—" began Lydia again.

"If you'd only listen instead of jumping to conclusions, I wasn't going to mention Uncle Arthur. What *I've* got to wire for, my good girl," said Toby, "is cash."

"How absurd," said Lydia. "We must have heaps to get home with—even after paying René twenty-five pounds to dig his mum's allotment. I'd certainly sooner wire anyone than go to horrible Mr. Dumbly for our fares; but even if Tante Adèle's turns out slightly more expensive than the Grand—and I shouldn't be at all surprised—we can still hitch-hike."

"Only there are all those I.O.U.s I left," said Toby.

2.

So completely had the experiences of the day obliterated all others, however recent, Lydia stared uncomprehendingly.

"At the pig-party," reminded Toby. "I can hardly leave the country without redeeming 'em."

All Preludes were conscientious about money. Lydia, after time for reflection, nodded.

"I'd forgotten; but of course you're right. How much did it come to?"

"Roughly a hundred quid. Mostly Bobo's. But there wasn't time to count, I just put I.O.U.s all round; so what they each ought to get exactly I'm not sure. It's a bit of a teaser." Toby paused. His situation was indeed in a minor way rather like William's faced by the prospect of returning the wreaths from the funeral. "There's another thing: I don't know the chaps' proper names."

"You said ours was Blackwood," recalled Lydia. "I wondered why."

"Aboriginal instinct," said Toby. "Never give away your name to a strange tribe." (This was actually the first time they'd ever discussed the events of that alarming night; to find that they could was rather a relief.) "I saw from the start they were pretty hairy-hocked."

"Poor Mrs. Pig-face! We don't know her name either," sighed Lydia. "Anyway, what did you put on the I.O.U.s?"

"Naturally Prelude," said Toby. "But even if I'd put Blackwood—"

"Naturally," agreed Lydia.

"It's still pretty difficult to know what to wire," said Toby. "Obviously one can't go into details."

"Obviously."

"And I'll have to pitch it good and strong. I suppose I'd better," meditated Toby, "say I'm in jail."

Unhappily Lydia watched her cousin try out one or two phrases on the back of the menu—such as *Jailed for espionage. Jailed for insult to General de Gaulle.* To the credit of her budding sense of reality none looked very convincing, particularly if to be relayed by an Italian butler over the telephone. It was Toby who was giving his romanticism a last fling; but even he, after trying out a reference to Devil's Island, paused to chew his pencil.

"Actually," said Toby, "not that I mean to rub it in, I thought I could bank on Uncle Arthur. —That's not true," he added honestly. "I wasn't thinking at all. I was just being a bloody little Robin Hood."

"I was being St. Joan," confessed Lydia. "And Cordelia. And Aramis . . ."

If Toby suppressed his own rôle as Porthos, it was as irrelevant.

"Let's face it," said Toby. "We've made pretty complete fools of ourselves all round."

"Not you," said Lydia. "I persuaded you."

"On the facts, I don't see what else you could have done," said Toby loyally.

"Only they weren't facts . . . What's really so awful is that William and Elizabeth were right. Like horrible Mr. Dumbly. Oh, Toby, are the old *always* going to be right?"

For the space of a silent minute both contemplated the prospect with failing hearts. Youth's illusion of omniscience must always be rubbed off sooner or later; so far as Toby and Lydia were concerned, it was being rather roughly sand-papered.

"They warned us," recalled Lydia, "not to get mixed up with *louche* parties . . ."

"Or lose our money," recalled Toby.

"Or have our bicycles stolen."

"Or fall for con-men."

"I don't think you could actually call René a con-man," said Lydia. "At least he owned up."

"We haven't seen any of those fivers back."

"He spent them all on a washing-machine for his mother—" began Lydia; and checked herself. "I suppose of course he didn't. He just fleeced us."

"Like a couple of lambs," said Toby. "Innocents abroad."

"That's what he called us," said Lydia. "Innocents . . ."

[167]

There was a long pause while Lydia refilled her cup and Toby emptied his glass.

"I suppose I'm being pretty innocent now," said Toby, "thinking I can touch m' dad for a hundred quid on the strength of an insult to General de Gaulle."

"Yes," said Lydia.

"I don't believe *debt of honour* would work either."

"Of course I don't know Uncle Wilfred very well," said Lydia, "but I shouldn't think so."

"An I.O.U.'s still an I.O.U."

"I know just how you feel," said Lydia.

"I expect your mother," said Toby cautiously, "may be a bit fed up with getting wires from us?"

"So we'd better not send it till tomorrow," said Lydia.

3.

Mrs. Prelude, after her good night's sleep, received it with calm, and indeed without much surprise. ("Some heartless person!" thought Mrs. Prelude. "Poor Lydia!") She was a soft touch in any case, also accustomed to the notion of cabling sums of money about Europe: all one had to do was telephone the Bank. "One hundred pounds, please," telephoned Mrs. Prelude, "to Miss Lydia Prelude, Crédit Lyonnaise, Chambérieu; then you send me something to sign . . ." "With pleasure, Mrs. Prelude," agreed a deferential managerial voice. "One hundred only?" "That's all she's asked for," explained Mrs. Prelude. "The good child!"

4.

Thus Toby was able, before he and Lydia set their faces homeward, to dispatch a registered envelope directed to Madame la Châtelaine, Le Château, Villeneuve-le-Duc. This was Lydia's suggestion, who felt Mrs. Pig-face would enjoy being addressed as a châtelaine. "She can hand it out," added Lydia. "Bobo and Blimps won't have forgotten what they're owed. All you need put is something like *mille mercis* . . ."

"And an address," said Toby firmly.

He never got his I.O.U.s back, however, and actually no more did Bobo or Peter or Blimps get their money back: Mrs. Armadale, as usual tight as a tick, upon opening the envelope vaguely assumed subscriptions to the Bal des Petits Lits Blancs, and a week later at Monte Carlo was quite surprised to see her table half empty. (Rough justice nonetheless; ninety per cent of the cash had been stolen from her by Bobo originally.) In any case Toby's conscience was cleared, and he was able to pay the staggering bill presented by Tante Adèle with milordish aplomb. (He still deplored Lydia's buying René a wrist-watch, but Lydia was stubborn; hadn't he at least owned up in time to save them making even worse fools of themselves?) René for his part saw the cousins onto the train with genuine tears in his eyes. Financial profit aside, he'd never been happier in his life than sitting under the elms, under the fairy-lights, with his high-class British pals . . .

"Never, never will I forget you!" swore René emotionally.

"I bet you won't," said Toby. In any case he was inoculated for life against con-men.

From behind his back René suddenly whipped half-a-dozen carnations wrapped in cellophane and pressed them into Lydia's hands.

"Let Mademoiselle remember me, if only so long as these poor blooms last!" begged René, more emotionally still. "*Au revoir*—for I cannot say *adieu!* The address of my aunt's *pension* is on the card: I hope you will recommend her."

5.

"But they're half dead already!" exclaimed Lydia indignantly, pulling the cellophane apart as the train gathered way.

"He's probably got another aunt who runs a flower-shop," said Toby. "Let it teach you to take a good look, my girl, when bouquets start hurtling over the foot-lights."

"Bouquets haven't hurtled for ages," said Lydia. "They're sent round." She reflected nonetheless. "Those plums weren't much either; I mean after we escaped from the pig-party."

"That suitcase you bought—" began Toby.

"I know," said Lydia quickly. "It isn't leather. But there's nothing wrong with my underthings. They're miraculous." —Suddenly she closed her eyes; for a moment, as behind their lids declining sunlight flooded a western window, the thought occurred that if she'd indeed identified the miracle promised her in the church with the *beau jubé,* then the Virgin had an unexpected sense of humour. But since Toby was an agnostic, Lydia refrained from describing how it felt to be gently kicked off from On High. "Actually I don't mind going home as much as I thought I should," decided Lydia, opening her eyes, "even to another ghastly family lunch with William and Elizabeth."

"My lot too," warned Toby.

Lydia, back to earth again, hesitated. "I think perhaps we'd better get Mother by herself first . . ."

"Absolutely," said Toby. "And if those carnations don't hold out buy another bunch in London."

"She won't be angry. She's too loving," said Lydia vaguely. "She'll forgive us . . ."

"But what for?" asked Toby reasonably. "It's not as though we'd done any damage . . ."

6.

Encouraged by which thought the cousins completed the rest of the journey in good spirits, and only because they spent so long buying carnations in Victoria Street missed the 10:10 from Marylebone to Chesham Bois. The 11:10 indeed got them to Chesham by noon; unfortunately for Lydia's and Toby's plan, there was no taxi at the station to save them a three-mile walk, and by the time they arrived the rest of Mrs. Prelude's luncheon-party was already assembled.

20

ELIZABETH AND HENRY, who had driven from the air-port, and William, who had driven from Bond Street, encountered each other practically on the threshold. William stared in surprise, not only at the sight of his sister, but even more at the sight of a man with her. He recovered his manners however before she had time to speak.

"Alistair? Nice to meet you," said William. "But I trust the Grecian shores didn't disappoint?"

"Henry," corrected Elizabeth, sensibly without lowering her voice. "Henry Alcott. —This is my antique-dealing brother William, darling. He puts on an act."

"Don't we all?" said Henry Alcott.

Elizabeth looked at him rather sharply, but turned to William again.

"And the Grecian shores are marvellous. We're flying back tonight."

"What a very van-Hoytish proceeding," said William. "Shall we all, do you suppose, be taking to aeroplanes just like busses? I look forward to meeting him. What about you, Alcock?"

"Alcott," said Henry.

"A rose by any name," apologized William, who hadn't seen Alice for thirteen days. "But we mustn't keep family lunch waiting while we idly chit-chat . . ."

It was at this point that Elizabeth slipped the silver-coin ring from her finger and into her bag. She felt she would prefer to announce her engagement to her mother first, and alone; certainly not in front of Mrs. Wilfred, who was there with her husband already.

2.

If William was surprised to see his sister, so had been Mrs. Prelude to see her brother-in-law; she'd fully expected him to renege on the plea of accumulated paper-work—his usual excuse even at Christmas. But he'd not only come; he brought a present.

"How very pretty!" exclaimed Mrs. Prelude, surveying the miniature obelisk with genuine if astonished appreciation. "Is it made of something?"

"You don't recognize it?"

"Spar," put in Mrs. Wilfred. "Wilfred and Arthur, when they were little boys, used to have such a fad for minerals! Surely Arthur told you how they went to the National Geological together?"

"No," confessed Mrs. Prelude.

"Wilfred told *me*," said Mrs. Wilfred cosily. "Didn't you, darling?"

For answer her husband patted her hand. —It struck Mrs. Prelude that there was something unusual about the Wilfreds altogether: an air of complacency in each other, even a honeymoon-ish air. But before she had time to examine the thought, in walked William and Elizabeth and a strange man. Evidently it was to be a day of surprises.

3.

What struck Elizabeth and William was that Mr. van Hoyt wasn't present. (Henry took Wilfred Prelude for him.) But there was time still, and each had other preoccupations.

"Mother, I've brought Henry Alcott," said Elizabeth. "We've been fellow-travellers in Greece."

"Where's Alice?" demanded William.

"Coming, darling," said Mrs. Prelude. —"How nice to meet one of my daughter's friends!" she added traditionally. "William, give Mr. Alcott a sherry. Uncle Wilfred's drinking whisky."

Henry, thus disabused as to Wilfred Prelude's identity, nevertheless asked for whisky too. Confronting his love's mother, brother, uncle, presumably aunt, expectant of a sister and cousin as well, he would actually have preferred brandy, but didn't see any.

Elizabeth said Alice would probably want gin. "It's not shellfish, dear," reassured Mrs. Prelude, to herself at least quite explicably, and showed Henry the obelisk. Since she still had it in her hand it was an obvious thing to do, one of those little social gestures so useful in breaking the social ice. Unfortunately William, always attracted to any bibelot, closed up before she could do more than explain that it was hand-carved out of natural spar. "How very misguided," said William. "Your Uncle Wilfred brought it me," said Mrs. Prelude. "Do I contradict myself? Very well, I contradict myself. Walt Whitman," said William. "Actually you've left out a word," corrected Elizabeth. "It's 'Very well, then.'" "I'm sure by now you've learnt always to verify your quotations," said William, raising his glass to Henry Alcott. "God bless us every one. Tiny Tim."

William Prelude observed that it was after one.

"But where are the children?" exclaimed Mrs. Wilfred. "Don't say they're going to be late! —Has anyone heard from them?" she added. "Bad Toby never sent so much as a post-card!"

Though the question was formally general, her eye was naturally on Mrs. Prelude, who answered with her usual placid smile.

"I have, dear. Three times."

"I suppose from Lydia?" said Mrs. Wilfred. "Girls are always more conscientious! What did she say?"

"Oh, just how much they were enjoying themselves on their bicycles," returned Mrs. Prelude.

The cousins had been right to trust her. It was sheer bad luck that Elizabeth, at that moment glancing through a window, spotted them panting up the drive on foot.

4.

Lacking Alice and Mr. van Hoyt, but with Henry Alcott and Uncle Wilfred unexpected substitutes, all eight places laid by Mrs. Prelude were filled. —Eight is a large number for lunch, in a staffless house; as on the day of the funeral, it was ham and tongue.

"Now let's tell each other everything that's been happening!" said Mrs. Wilfred brightly. "Toby and Lydia to begin!"

Each glanced swiftly towards Mrs. Prelude. Her hug of welcome, almost crushing the carnations, had reassured in itself; now a tender smile and nod affirmed that she hadn't, never would, split. "*Later!*" mouthed Mrs. Prelude silently. Toby drew a deep breath; Lydia returned to eating ham.

"I suppose the most exciting thing," said Toby, "was when my bike packed up."

"I'm very glad to hear it," said Mrs. Wilfred. "Those brakes were a mum's nightmare. How did you manage, darling?"

"I hired another, Mamma."

"Lydia's was new," observed Elizabeth.

"Last birthday," reminded Mrs. Prelude. "Nearly a year ago."

"Actually I gave it away," said Lydia, "to a Youth Hostel for orphans where they were short on bikes."

Elizabeth's look of disbelief was so explicit, Mrs. Wilfred, who reciprocally disliked her niece, not quite tactfully intervened.

"At least they didn't get their *money* stolen! —Have you brought back a penny, darling?"

"Eighteen-and-six," said Toby. "At least, I suppose nine-and-three's Lydia's."

"Toby kept the purse," explained Lydia. "We saw some wonderful churches."

"Mother, are you certain you asked her?" demanded William.

"Alice? Of course I did," said Mrs. Prelude. "Just a few days ago. The day Mr. van Hoyt came. I was so sorry she wouldn't stay to meet him!"

"How very odd," said Elizabeth. The name van Hoyt at last pronounced, however, she asked the question uppermost in several minds. "Didn't you say he'd be here, Mother?"

"Oh, I still expect him," said Mrs. Prelude cheerfully. "He's such a very old acquaintance, he'll probably just walk in . . . Why not telephone her at her friends', darling? Say it's a cold lunch."

William pushed back his chair and left the table.

"What churches?" asked Elizabeth.

"Well, the one at Villeneuve-le-Duc was the best," said Lydia. "It had a *beau jubé*. I—I lit a candle . . ."

"If she's still driving that absurd jeep I expect it's broken down," said Mrs. Wilfred. "What on earth's a *jubé*?"

"A rood-screen," supplied Wilfred Prelude unexpectedly.

—His wife smiled encouragement: she'd been wishing he'd chat more, he was as silent as Elizabeth's young man; but a family gathering was still strange to him, and Toby, who saw Lydia on the verge of tears, had decided to take the war into the enemy camp.

"Now let's hear Cousin Elizabeth's and Mr. Alcott's experiences," said Toby courteously.

"Only of sun and sea," said Elizabeth. "Sun very hot and sea very blue . . ."

"You met bathing?" asked Mrs. Prelude of Henry. —As the first young man Elizabeth had ever brought home, she would normally have felt a quite passionate interest in him, but there was much on her mind.

"Actually in Athens," said Henry. "At the Embassy. We were both signing the Book."

It was the tale they had invented together in the plane on the way home, partly as a private joke, partly as a sop to Elizabeth's mother, for whom Elizabeth didn't scruple to admit a protective affection. —She was happy to recognize a fringe success; Mrs. Prelude looked pleased.

"Your father always signed the Book wherever we went. Even just consuls': he said it encouraged them."

"I think all consuls are oafs," said Lydia huskily.

"Nonsense, dear; you've never had anything to do with one," rebuked Mrs. Prelude. "Well, William?"

"She isn't there," reported William. "Her father's ill. Don't wait for me, you won't mind, while I telephone Oxford?"

"Of course not, darling. Give her my love," said Mrs. Prelude. —"And so I suppose you went on little jaunts to the beach together?"

Henry Alcott nodded. The further invention, of a second chance encounter at Morning Service, he was by now too uneasy to recall. The terms mother, father, cousin, uncle, brother, the constant dears and darlings, had begun to buzz about his ears like a swarm of mosquitoes. Even the obelisk so innocently proffered by Mrs. Prelude, and now set prominently beside her plate, was a source of uneasiness: just such misguided artifacts—here he felt a brief sympathy with brother William—had adorned the mantelpieces of a home from which it had been his one successful ambition to escape. (Not all indeed of spar, mostly of porcelain defaced by the arms of such watering-places as Bournemouth, Ramsgate and Bognor Regis. The view of Brixham was painted on a shark's egg.) It was still to an aunt that he owed immediate relief, as Mrs. Wilfred, however unwittingly, covered his silence by the remark that it was always nice to have a man with one while bathing, in case of big waves.

"Henry swims like a fish," agreed Elizabeth. "He taught me the butterfly stroke."

"I thought you learned it ages ago," said Lydia, "from that man at the Marylebone Baths."

It was a rash observation, as drawing her sister's fire afresh.

"What Youth Hostel for Orphans?" enquired Elizabeth —and both Toby and Lydia knew she was perfectly capable of checking up. "Is there one at Villeneuve-le-Duc?"

"No, it was after," said Lydia.

"After St. Emilien, with *beau jubé*," explained Toby, "we were led on to St. Georges and St. Barsac—I'm sorry if it sounds rather like a wine-list—both with remarkable fonts. Were you and Mr. Alcott led on to Delphi?"

"No," admitted Elizabeth. "The sun and the sea—"

"Were too hot and too blue?"

"Toby and I saw a château as well," put in Lydia virtuously.

At which point William returned looking white as a sheet.

5.

"Darling!" exclaimed Mrs. Prelude in alarm. "Is Alice ill too? Couldn't you speak to her?"

"Not to Alice," articulated William, "only to her daddy. Alice was too upset."

"Good gracious, if her father can answer the telephone," said Mrs. Prelude, "what about?"

"Breaking off our engagement," said William bleakly. "She was too upset to tell me herself, so her daddy had to do it for her. Don't mind if I don't have cheese."

He closed the door behind him with exaggerated care. Mrs. Prelude gazed at it compassionately.

"Poor boy! Should I go to him, do you think?"

"No, Mother," said Elizabeth.

"Or telephone Alice myself? It may be just something silly he's done—like not answering a note."

"No, Mother," repeated Elizabeth. "He won't realize it yet, but William has had a lucky escape."

"I agree," said Lydia. "Toby and I often wondered whether there was anything we could do about it."

"Of course she was immensely pretty," reflected Mrs. Wilfred, "but in a way such an *old-fashioned* girl . . . Do go on, Mr. Alcott, about Greece."

The door opened again.

"I forgot," said William. "Van Hoyt's there."

"What!" exclaimed Mrs. Prelude.

"In Oxford. Alice's daddy's been showing him round the quads."

"Then he's able to get about?" asked Mrs. Wilfred, with an easy switch of interest. "He hasn't been really seriously ill?"

"One thing we can all bet on," said Elizabeth, "is that Alice has been showing him round too."

6.

She had spoken almost without thinking, simply out of the old habit of twitting William: but the words, as their implications developed, and not least in her own mind, produced a considerable pause. Mrs. Wilfred was the first to break it.

"But I thought you said she didn't meet him?" she asked her sister-in-law.

"She didn't," said Mrs. Prelude. "She drove straight away in her jeep."

"I thought it odd," said Elizabeth.

William walked out again.

"I think," said Lydia, "she just hung about outside and picked him up."

"Lydia!"

"Well, it's just what she would do, Mother."

"He'd certainly be a great catch," reflected Mrs. Wilfred. "And marrying for money sometimes turns out very happily. Of course he must be much *older* than Alice—?"

"I never thought of him as old at all," said Mrs. Prelude. "But yes, older than Alice . . ."

"Girls can't have everything," said her sister-in-law. "And now, my dear, nice as it's been—as lunch here always is!—we must really take Toby home. —Your father's got a surprise for you," she added, to Toby. "A bonfire and fireworks, to celebrate!"

7.

William had returned to London: Elizabeth and Henry were driving to the airport. Both were rather silent; it suddenly seemed rather foolish, rather a waste of money, to have flown back from Greece. "Obviously *not* the time," said Henry, "for announcing betrothals. Not with your brother's in ruins about his head . . ." "Obviously not," agreed Elizabeth. "I was very glad you didn't . . . —I can't wait to be in the sea again."

"Nor I," said Henry.

"You swim like a fish," said Elizabeth.

8.

Alone with her mother in the empty dining-room—the table melancholy as a deserted *table d'hôte,* the scent of carnations heavy on the air—Lydia put her arms round Mrs. Prelude's neck; then withdrew to make painful confession at last.

"Toby wants me to tell you straight away," opened Lydia, "it was his fault we lost our money."

Mrs. Prelude achieved a wan smile.

"The money doesn't matter, darling."

"And we're both terribly, terribly sorry if our wires upset you. Both Toby and I are sorry with all our hearts. We—I—just made a terrible mistake."

"As I did," sighed Mrs. Prelude. "As I did . . . You really went to look for Father?"

Lydia nodded. "If you don't mind, I'd rather not tell you about it; but Elizabeth and William and—and everyone, were right."

"No; don't tell me," said Mrs. Prelude. "I'm sure you've been very good, brave children."

She sighed again, however; so deeply, Lydia felt an anxious pang.

"We didn't do any damage, Mother?"

"There's the telephone," said Mrs. Prelude. "Answer it for me, will you, dear? I don't know why, I'm rather tired."

She was too tired even to finish clearing the table. While Lydia was out of the room she simply sat, hands loosely clasped in her lap, remembering, and musing, and blaming herself. "I deserve nothing better," Mrs. Prelude told herself obscurely. "Poor Lydia, poor Toby!" Only at the sound of her daughter's returning step did she summon the energy to pick up a plate and tip from it a rind of cheese . . .

"It was Professor Harvill," reported Lydia, "but he didn't say any more about Alice. He just asked," reported Lydia, with some indignation, "whether it would be etiquette-wise acceptable if he came to tea. Of course I told him you were much too tired, Mother, to see *anyone*."

During thirty years of married life Mrs. Prelude's sole manifestation of independence had been when flying to sit in the tail. Her brief widowhood had been dominated by

William and Elizabeth and Miss Champney and Miss Hume. Lydia's and Toby's chivalrous excursion had but strengthened, so to speak, every loyal bond. It was quite surprising, in the circumstances, how swiftly Mrs. Prelude was at the telephone herself ringing back Oxford.